Frank Middleton

Uberto

The errors of the heart - a drama in five acts

Frank Middleton

Uberto
The errors of the heart - a drama in five acts

ISBN/EAN: 9783337343712

Printed in Europe, USA, Canada, Australia, Japan

Cover: Foto ©Andreas Hilbeck / pixelio.de

More available books at **www.hansebooks.com**

UBERTO;

OR,

THE ERRORS OF THE HEART.

~~~~~~~~~~~~

A DRAMA

IN FIVE ACTS.

BY FRANK MIDDLETON,

~~~~~~~~~~~~~~~

New York:
BRADLEY & WHITE,
STATIONERS AND PRINTERS,
23 WILLIAM STREET.

————

1867.

DRAMATIS PERSONÆ.

———◆———

UBERTO, a young Neapolitan Baron.

VITELLI of Castello, his friend.

JEROME FORLI, a neighboring Baron.

CAPTAIN BELLAMORI, of the Lances.

MATTEO ARCANO, Steward to Uberto.

CHARLES, Duke of Savoy and King of Cyprus.

CHANCELLOR MANCINI.

1ST COUNCILLOR.

2ND COUNCILLOR.

3RD COUNCILLOR.

MARCO FRACCO, a Savoyard.

PIETRO, a Savoyard.

REGINA, daughter of Forli.

FRANCESCA, daughter of Mancini.

BONITA, daughter of Pietro.

1ST SOLDIER.

2ND SOLDIER.

3RD SOLDIER.

TWO RETAINERS OF VITELLI.

A DOCTOR.

A SERVANT.

AN OFFICER.

A BAND OF FREE COMPANIONS.

UBERTO;

OR, THE

ERRORS OF THE HEART

———◦◦◦———

ACT I.

SCENE 1.—*The outside of a Castle.—A trumpet is heard—
Enter from one side two retainers of Vitelli, and from the
other Matteo Arcano, the steward of Uberto.*

FIRST RETAINER. Whose castle may this be?

ARCANO. His Lordship's castle.

1ST R. His Lordship's castle! That is information.

2ND R. 'Tis not such information as will pass
With him who sent us hither.

FIRST R.—Gentle Sir,
If that, indeed, thy quality be such,
Inform us speedily whose towers are these,
For we have that to say unto their lord,
In case he be the one we take him for,
Which a wise man would rather help than hinder.

2ND R. For if thou wilt not speak, why, then, we'll make thee.

ARCANO. Good gentlemen, what I have said is true;
This is his Lordship's castle; all the neighborhood
Well knows his name and dignity; but I.
I am his representative; my name
Is Matteo Arcano.

1ST R. Bless the mark!

2ND R. Then after all we have acquired some knowledge.

ARCANO. I, Matteo Arcano, am responsible—

1ST R. If your responsibility will deign
To give his Lordship's name, 'tis all we ask.

2ND R. Or say if Lord Uberto keeps this castle.

ARCANO. Why, truly, sir, he does. I did not say
That I was master here.

1ST R. We pray your dignity will condescend
To tell your lord that some one waits beyond,
Asking his hospitality, a friend
Of days gone by, an old companion.

ARCANO. Who?

1st R. Vitelli of Castello. Look beyond!
His escort waits beside that gentle hill.

Arcano. Vitelli of Castello!

2nd R. Thou hast said it.

Arcano. Waits beyond!

1st R. That is the whole disclosure.

Arcano. Then, gentlemen, I will inform my lord
His old companion asks admission. Truly
There is a press of business on my shoulders
I did not think of. (*Going out.*)

2nd R. Hark you, Mister Steward,
When we do meet again be more considerate,
For we are men o' the world, I promise you.

1st R. Yes, truly, men o' the world, that are we.
(*All exeunt.*)

Scene 2.—*A Hall.—Enter from one side Uberto with retainers; from the other, Arcano, walking backwards and bowing, as he leads in Vitelli, with the retainers who appeared before, and others.*

Uberto. Welcome, Vitelli, to our ancient halls!
Thy presence is a boon which in itself,
Apart from previous friendship's added charm,
Would prove consoling to the lonely hours
Of dwellers in the woods. Long years ago
We parted, promising to meet again.
Now, that short intercourse which boyhood's heart
Felt still more short, shall be again renewed;
And manhood's judgment crowning early sympathy
Shall prove the instincts of the heart divine.

Vitelli. Signor Uberto, I am one of those
Who boast not much of motives, nor take pride
In shaping out their conduct and their course,
In nice attractive patterns of virtue;
But yet at times I do a model act,
Without design or skill, and yet so perfect
As to surprise the critics. Thus, to-day
I have redeemed my pledge of boyish faith.
(*Exeunt all attendants.*)

Uberto. Thou hast redeemed it, and art yet the same.
I think I can detect in this thy speech
The same odd biting candor as of old—
'Tis but the humor of an honest heart
Which chooses to put forth its high resolves,
Not merely in their own pure spotless grace,
But throws them forward with a playful force,
Relieving the monotony of virtue
With some fine touches of imagination.

Vitelli. Be never sure, Uberto, without seeing—
The theory that's formed amidst the woods

ERRORS OF THE HEART.

Is not the knowledge learned among the cities.
Our solitary thoughts are our worst foes;
Painting the universe in their own colors,
They lie in what they tell us.   The old maxim
Put forward by the sage, of "Know Thyself,"
Might be amended into " Know the World."
    UBERTO.   What is this world that is unknown to me,
And that thou knowest so well?
    VITELLI.   A paradise
To those who look from far with youthful eyes.
For me, it is a place has served me well;
I love it dearly, though not tenderly.
But come—in three days' time I must depart.
Are there no sports, no pranks, no recreations,
No mysteries, no mischiefs that may cheer us?
What men, what women, constitute this life,
So still, old-fashioned and obscure ?
    UBERTO.   Alas !
My state is poor—my court is circumscribed.
Here are no joys except for those like me,
Who look no further than the ancient woods
That intervene betwixt the world and them.
There's not in Naples' bounds a poorer baron;
There's not in Italy a slenderer train.
    VITELLI.   Hast thou no force, no officers, no household ?
    UBERTO.   Two officers comprise my following.
First, Captain Bellamori, my commander,
Who heads my forces when I go to war.
    VITELLI.   What may thy forces be ?
    UBERTO.   Just none at all.
But when I have them he is to command.
    VITELLI.   He's a Free Lance, mayhap ?
    UBERTO.   He's a Free Lance;
    VITELLI.   And likely he's as full of dignity
As though his name were Sforza, Duke of Milan.
    UBERTO.   Why, thou dost know him then ?
    VITELLI.   I know his family.
    UBERTO.   His family !
    VITELLI.   Oh ! yes, I know the Lances.
'Tis to be thought that he is like the rest.
    UBERTO.   So much for him.   Then Matteo Arcano,
The steward of my household, is the next.
    VITELLI.   I've noticed him.   He is both old and faithful;
Fills his important post with fitting pride,
And thinks that spot the centre of the world
Where he presides—
    UBERTO.   Then thou dost know him too ?
    VITELLI.   I've seen such oft'.   There's nothing new on earth,
These are but studies I have met before.
    UBERTO.   Something remains thou hast not met before.
    1*

Vitelli. What's that?

Uberto.   A mystery—

Vitelli. Why, then, that's something.

Uberto. It shall not be a mystery to thee.
I have a secret here that thou shalt know,
It is the secret of my sweet content.
It tells why I am happy in these woods,
These ruined halls.

Vitelli. Uberto, keep thy secret.
When I wish secrets told me I buy them;
And what we buy we value. Confidence
Is a bad bargain for both sides at once,
For while one gives what can not be regained,
The other has no profit.

Uberto.   I'll be trustful.
The bosom, thronged with secret pain or joy,
Bounds when a heart, though ev'n untried, draws near.
And longs to make it partner of its throbs.

Vitelli. So be it; thou wilt have it so.

Uberto.   But, then,
I'll ask some secret from thee in return.

Vitelli. Now, thou art jesting.

Uberto.   And we'll make a wager;
And he whose tale is poorer shall pay forfeit.

Vitelli. Well, I will wager this (*his dagger*) and lose it too.

Uberto. And I'll give thee a horse if thou prevail.

Vitelli. My secrets are worth swords and horses.

Uberto.   Then, to-morrow
We'll go to that far castle in the woods;
There are some friends shall judge between us.

Vitelli.   Now,
This seems to me a miserable means
Of weak invention to contrive a pastime.
But let it go.   Do we set out to-morrow?

Uberto. To-morrow we set forth for yonder castle.

Vitelli. And each shall tell his tale.

Uberto.   And one pay forfeit.
Meantime we'll spend the hours as best we may.
Come, walk with me around my little realm,
I'll make thee partner in my sovereign sway,
And lord of all my ruins. (*Exit.*)

Vitelli.   Is it possible
That men of mind and form matured can stoop
To little childish wayside games?   Poor simpleton,
That hid'st thy head and think'st thou art not seen.
The nature of this deeply-hidden secret
Is published in his face, his gait, his manner.
But let me once forget what I have been,
And for a day put on simplicity,
And may no profit, no advantage, lurking,

As yet unseen, with sudden glitter lure me
To do that which I should not.   Keep away
Such temptings and for once I shall be pure.   (*Exit.*)

SCENE 3.—*The same.—Enter Matteo Arcano, Steward of the
    Castle.*
MATT. A great position hath its days of pain,
But 'tis such days as this that try one's genius.
I, Matteo Arcano, am the man
To take responsibility with ease
And turn it into profit.   Now, to prove me,
Comes to us Lord Vitelli, a poor noble
Stripped of his patrimony years ago,
By war or some bad chance, no matter what.
Here my responsibility falls short.
He is a youth of a most caustic tongue;
And this has to be borne in such a jest
As not to lower in aught the dignity
Of those who bear it, and for this nice action,
This equipoise of dangerous elements,
I am responsible.
Now, may Heaven keep me from all gusts of war!
Some angry wind blows here.   Our brawny captain,
I'd not be manager of Naples Kingdom
And be responsible for such as he.
                    (*Enter* CAPTAIN BELLAMORI.)
Brave Bellamori, what is it disturbs thee?
    BELL. The curse of peace pursue me, but I hate him!
    ARC. Whom, good captain?
    BELL.   Whom! our visitor;
He has such words and ways as suit me not.
    ARC. Oh! pray inform me how he hath offended?
    BELL. Coming across the court I met them both—
Him and our master—but this very instant;
And while Uberto dreamily passed on,
Vitelli stopped, and with a mocking eye
Of sharp intelligence, asked how I did;
And when I answered civilly, he questioned
About my forces, asked where they were lodged,
How many they were all, both horse and foot,
And why it was they did not man the walls
To do him honor.   Thus he questioned me,
Knowing I was the only soldier here.
    ARC. Dismiss these thoughts, good soldier, from thy breast.
Bethink thee of the courtesy that's due
Unto the honored guest within our walls;
And think of my responsibility—
    BELL. Which weighs no more with me than doth a rivet
Upon my helmet's clasp.
    ARC.   Thou art uncourteous.

Thy speech is like a soldier's life, good captain—
Violent and short; but come, we'll take some wine;
To raise or end a quarrel wine is potent.
    BELL. Some it makes garrulous, and some makes cautious.
Thou knowest when I take wine that I take caution;
Free ebullition is my regularity.
When I am crabbed, cold, I've taken wine;
But it shall cost some wine to slake my ire.
(*Matteo draws forth a table with glasses, and they sit down*).
Think for a moment how I am insulted.
Thou know'st that in this peace-rid spot of ours
We have *no* troops, and I am called their captain.
Vitelli asks me all about their numbers,
And the expenses for their proper care.
    ARC. Good captain, let me question thee a little!
    BELL. Peace rot thy bones! but do *thou* answer *me*?
    MATT. As my responsibility allows.
    BELL. Tell thy opinion of the Lord Uberto?
    MATT. The Lord Uberto is a gentleman
Who aims at honor in his ev'ry act;
He sees not much outside him, for his eyes
Are ever turned within; himself he judges
By a too rigid rule—all others gen'rously.
In his own judgment he is bad enough,
While truly there's none better on the earth!
    BELL. Tell always truth like this, and I'm your captain.
    MATT. What more—
    BELL. Now, thy opinion of Vitelli.
    MATT. I'm not responsible for Lord Vitelli;
But he would seem to me to be well-bred,
A gentleman, accomplished, practised, courtly—
    BELL. Slashed sleeves and handsome doublet, Spanish sword,
With boots to ride in—night-cap when he sleeps.
    MATT. In truth I think so. What, what canst thou mean?
    BELL. And now we have his *character*. I know thee;
Thou wouldst not say it, but wouldst have it said.
Thou speak'st as to a child, masking with trifles
The thing that thou wouldst hide. If I were asked,
I'd say he is Uberto's very opposite.
There is no honor and no soundness in him.
If such a man commanded a great post,
Which ev'ry State in Italy had sworn him
And paid him to defend, he'd hang the man
That would not call him honest; but when tried
He'd sell it to the devil for a dukedom,
If that, indeed, be what he seeks.
    ARC.   Oh, hush!
This judgment is ill-founded, rash and wrong;
The gentleman has merely a sharp wit.
    BELL. I have a dagger sharper than his wit.

ARC. (rising) Now, may Heaven shield us! but he comes this way
Let not thy heroic but ill-timed valor
Tempt thee to aught that we should both regret
Enter Vitelli.
VIT. (*aside*) I left him poring o'er the idle brook,
Forgetting. in his profitless abstraction,
A world which scarcely feels his presence in it.
So let him dream, but I must see my way,
And seeing, profit by my knowledge.
Steward,
As I am vested with authority,
I order thee prepare a sumptuous feast.
We shall make music in this pulseless place,
Until the antiquated silence laughs
With new-found life made by our revelry.
Captain, send forth thy troops to scour the woods
For meat to make our feast and guests to eat it.
BELL. My troops are not in marching mood to-day.
VIT. Are they not disciplined ?
BELL.　　　　　　　　　　Their discipline
Is of the perfect kind, immaculate—
VIT. With more of law and order than vitality.
BELL. In part that's true, but some of them, I'd warn you
Have more vitality than law or order.
VIT. These are the household troops that show this fire ?
BELL. The curse of peace upon us! Truth is truth.
If thou wouldst have it, our whole force is small.
VIT. How many truly are there, horse and foot ?
BELL. I have not writ them in my register.
Attack our castle and thou'lt find a host.
VIT. If I guess right, the foot exceeds the horse—
Exceeds the horse by one, and that's thyself :
The foot exceeds and thou art in excess.
BELL. The gentleman I serve has friends enough
To meet his enemies, and these are few.
It needs no troops to meet the gibing tongue ;
It needs no swords to match the scoffer's weapons.
VIT. We once had such a tinselled Hercules
Within my father's halls. He was rude spoken,
And daily would fight battles with his tongue ;
But when the day of danger came, and all
Took to their swords and threw away the scabbards,
Our hero threw away his scabbard, too,
But one thing he neglected—
BELL.　　　　　　　　What was that ?
VIT. The drawing of the weapon.
BELL. (*drawing*)　　　　　Here's a difference.
VIT. A *difference* indeed. Put up thy dagger,
I'd not draw steel on such a one as thou.
(*Vitelli gets behind the table.*)

MATT. Oh! peace, good captain, list to those kind words;
He would not draw his steel on such as thou.
  BELL. Take back those words of thine.
  VIT.   Put up thy dagger.
    They move round the table, Bellamori after Vitelli.)
  BELL. This shall not save thee, thou shalt eat thy words.
  MATT. Oh! my responsibility, alas!
What can be done? Come hither, Lord Uberto!
Uberto!
  (*Bellamori makes a stroke at Vitelli, who defends himself
    with a chair. He moves against the table which falls with
    a crash. Uberto rushes in.*)
  UB. The sound came hence. Here is some noisy jest.
  VIT. The captain and myself have had a jest,
Which, truth to say, was something like a tilt.
The captain has a sort of *cutting* manner,
When he makes answer to a pleasantry.
Behold you, sir, that brilliant repartee
He launched just now upon me?
  UB.   What! his dagger!
I did not think thy temper was so dark.
In truth, thy aspect is but ill-becoming,
Standing, with knife in hand, in my own presence,
To slay my friend and guest. Tis not our custom,
Though we are poor, to slay our friends or guests,
Or to keep butchers in our father's hall.
Captain, put up the knife. Go not, Arcano,
There's something here that must be further known.
  VIT. How a mere jest doth probe their stupid life!
This is what comes of living in the woods.
The callous texture which in jostling crowds
Clothes one in useful armor here is wanting;
And in its stead a tenderness is found,
An unsophisticated sensitiveness,
Eager but stupid, vigilant but futile,
Which very much disgusts one.
  UB. to ARC. What were ye both about e'er this did happen?
  ARC. My lord, we were conversing.
  BELL.   Drinking, too;
Sir, we were drinking—he's responsible.
  VIT. (*aside*) There's the best point that hath been made to-day.
  UB. What was your conversation?
  ARC.   Of thy merits.
I said, for my part, that my lord was virtuous.
Did I not say so, Captain?
  UB.   Pass that by.
What other conversation did ye hold?
  ARC. We also spoke about our noble guest.
I said, for my part, all that one may say
When estimable persons are in question.

Vit. (*aside*) Give me the woods for pungency, hereafter!
Arc.   Did I not say so, Captain, on thy truth?
Bell.   Upon my truth, thou didst say some such lie.
Vit. (*aside*) The play of nature here can't hide itself:
Ev'n when it tries it fails—and thus we find it
Strong as the breeze, transparent as the air.
Come, tell me, Captain, what thou saidst of me.
  Bell.   Ask of the witness—if he say not truth,
Then thou and I are wronged, and I'll correct him.
  Arc.   My Lord, he spoke of our good guest as one
Most worthy of suspicion, in whose company
A vigilant suspicion would be wise.
  Ub.   Suspicion in my house hath never been.
  Vit.   Suspicion, my dear friend, is very good;
Better at times than a judicial process.
  Ub.   Suspicion in my breast hath never lodged;
Suspicion near my person shall not stay.
Sure sign of thoughts diseased, it wanders forth
To make the evil that it would expose.
'Tis possible to bear the ills of life—
But with a morbid mind to see them come,
And multiply them, though they be not real—
This is a sort of sad and wretched wisdom
Which I abjure for ever, and bestow
In full enjoyment to the evil one.
Better a thousand times to be deceived
Than bear within one's breast this active poison
Extracting venom from the goods of life,
And making all the ranges of our thoughts
Replete with foulness.   Captain, we must part.
  Vit. (*aside*) What a dogmatic piece of speculation!
  Bell.   If thou sayest "part," that means that I must go,
And the last vigorous vestige of old times
Is gone and left ye.   Ye are hopeless now.
Thank heaven that there are wars in Italy!
The German's eye with longing lustful glance
Still rests as ever on Italian fruits.
Listen at night, and when on Northern winds
Come clamorous sounds of war—amidst their fury
Is Bellamori knocking.   (*Exit.*)
  Vit. (*aside*) What a fine frenzy in a mercenary!
Withal, an auctioneer may do with him
What many a man of weight might stagger at—
And that's to knock him down.
  Ub.   Steward, provide him with all things he needs.
                     (*Exit Matteo.*)
Is it not fearful malice, friend Vitelli?
  Vit.   Thou hast dismissed thy army for my sake.
  Ub. Such causeless, wicked and absurd suspicion
I have not seen before.

Vɪᴛ.   It makes me wonder :
If I would injure thee, I know not how.
      Uв. Apart from that, I feel more high assurance
That if thou couldst thou wouldst not—it is time
To think of our excursion through the forest.   (*Exeunt.*)

Sᴄᴇɴᴇ 4.—*A Court and Garden at the Castle of Jerome Forli.
        Enter Jerome and his daughter Regina.*
      Jᴇʀ. 'Twere well, my daughter, if the ceaseless wars,
Which ever vex our fair ill-fated land,
Had not so claimed my action that I might
Bestow upon thy culture that good care
Needed by those who feel no mother's hand.
Too much, too much has Jerome Forli's home
Been used to feverish counsels, anxious plots,
And all those enterprises which so tend
To clog the ways of peace. 'Twere well, indeed,
Had I not so intensely strained my sight
With gazing at engrossing images,
Which brought but turbulence, or else delusion,
As to o'erlook the flower within my home,
Which grew beneath my eyes, without my knowledge,
Giving out sweetness undeserved to him
Who cared not that its beauty might be spoiled
And blasted by the rudeness of the time !
If thou art good, my daughter, thy good angel
Has offered to thy view some pattern
More lovely than my grim and wilful ways.
If thou hast faults which uncorrected nature
And ill inheritance may have bestowed,
I claim the authorship and the neglect.
      Rᴇɢ. I do not think so meanly of my father
As to regret the model he has given.
I have his honor and his pride of race,
His firmness, his adventure—
      Jᴇʀ.   Ah ! my girl,
These are not virtues that thou just hast named.
I thought them virtues 'till I reached this age ;
Now the serener evening of my life
Gives them a boding aspect. It were better
Arrest their growth if other good endowments
Attend them not, for now I must confess
That merely selfishness is their first source ;
Virtue begins by curbing of one's self.
      Rᴇɢ. These are not self, they wear a nobler front.
Can honor, can good faith, can truth be " self?"
Can courage, chivalry or love be " self?"
      Jᴇʀ. What else is love but selfishness supreme,
Which boasts itself to be supreme devotion ?
Fancy must have an idol it can worship,

Not for the idol's pleasure, but its own.
The one we fancy may not fancy us.
Is it unselfish to pay homage still
By tiring out as men did Jupiter?
It is the sense of duty that makes virtue.
Let Fancy owe to duty some allegiance,
And its desire may be a holy flame.
But if the fancy merely is our guide,
Then it may prove repulsion in the end
And hatred, or at best a deep mistake,
Sweet while it lasts, but which we needs must break.
   REG. Texts taken from the volume of old age,
Harsh interpretations of kind oracles,
Ye don't apply where mutual love is found,
Where love is both a pleasure and a debt,
A privilege and a duty. Pardon me,
These words of boldness—pardon me, my father!
Although our home be sweet and well-beloved;
Although the grand old Appenines, high crowned
With classic woods, so green, yet venerable;
Although these plains, rich as the evening skies
That bend above them—all, though all combine
To make our home more like a painter's dream
Than what the common mind would dare aspire to;
Yet there's a grimness which will not depart,
Yet there's a longing which will not be quenched—
   JER. There are no scenes more beautiful than this,
And no events in the great world beyond
Worthy a maiden's curiosity.
I've known that world, and in it borne my part.
Here in this home, too beautiful for me,
I am retired for life. And thou, my daughter,
Hope and delight of my old age, why is it
That this hot blood which I have thus subdued
Must, even in the females of our race,
Need discipline? Believe a father's word:
These are the happiest moments of thy life,
If thou art but content.
   REG.   Why not have ceremony?
A little court with all its forms, observances,
Its fêtes, its gay but innocent displays?
   JER. Gauds, gauds, I'll none of them; from them I fled.
When thou art married then the world is open.
   REG. *When I am married!*—sweet but awful words,
The heralds of a change which maiden's mind
Pictures so fairly, yet a change how solemn!
And if this e'er should be, if I should leave
My father and my home, why should I now
Disturb his spirit with my rash requests?
   JER. Regina, canst thou count for me the times
  2

Our neighbor baron has been here this month?
   Reg. I well remember them, they have been twenty.
   Jer. 'Tis well,—when I set eyes upon a man,
Gentle but fearless, moderate but constant,
Warm in his nature, studious of justice,
There is no treasure I would not bestow him.
Such is Uberto. If you love each other
It is the dearest wish my heart can hold.
If it is merely the attractive form
And not the inner excellence that wins thee,
I would not wager on thy constancy.
   Reg. How shall I answer thee? am I to speak?
   Jer. Make answer—no reserve—I am thy father.
Dost thou love him?
   Reg.   This, then, is my answer:
Uberto is my choice—him do I prize;
And when I change, I'm blind unto myself.
                Enter Servant.
My Lord, Signor Uberto and a stranger
Of noble presence have but now arrived,
And seek admittance.   (*Exit Servant.*)
   Jer.   Let them come—a stranger
Of noble presence! His presence is not asked for.
Are there not wars and councils where his nobleness
Might be more serviceable?
Enter Uberto and Vitelli.   *Uberto kneels and kisses Re-*
     gina's hand.
   Ub. Sweet lady, noble friend, I ask for pardon,
That, through affection, which will oft presume
To break through laws that coldness would respect,
I have, with hopeful error, contravened
The law of your seclusion—but wherever
Uberto's feet are not forbid to tread,
Vitelli of Castello there may enter.
   Jer. Vitelli of Castello! I remember
Thy father, Signor, in the days gone by
Ere I got sickened with the ways of war.
(*Uberto and Regina draw apart and seem engaged in con-*
   versation while Jerome and Vitelli are speaking together.)
   Vit. The images reflected in his life
Are courage and misfortune. To these images
The meditations of my youth were drawn.
   Jer. And meditation hath so fashioned thee
As to imbue thee with the self-same spirit
To meet the self-same fate?
   Vit.   In part, sir, yes;
But I have found some wisdom in my struggles;
And if misfortune choose to stay with me,
Then shall contentment bear her company;
And if old age, meanwhile should come the way,

Amongst them all I shall make room for virtue.

JER. Why this is excellent and wholesome language.
At thy age, sir, I had no virtue in me,
But thought of castles to be sacked—sometimes
I thought of worse—my faults lie heavy on me,
War and its decorations, in my eyes,
Seem but a graveyard decked with foppery.

VIT. Believe me, sir, *I* hate it—'tis but duty
That makes me draw a most unwilling sword,
In an unsought-for argument.

REGINA. (*Laughing to Uberto.*)
                                        Uberto,
Tell me once more the story. The poor Captain,
Our only warlike representative
Has left us to our own unskilled defence.
Tell me what gibe it was that tried his temper.

UBERTO. Vitelli will inform us—Noble sir, (*to Jerome*)
Know that my officer hath drawn his dagger
Upon my guest Vitelli, for some jest—

JER. And didst thou not dismiss him?

UB.   Sir, I did.

JER. 'Twas well.

UB.   Vitelli, say what was the jest.

VIT. I said the Milanese could not make armor.

JER. The Milanese! It was a trying thing
Unto a man like him. The Milanese!
The best of armor makers in the world,
But I care not.

VIT.   And I cared not, good sir.
In truth I scarcely knew. I trod by chance
Upon most dangerous ground.

JER.   The Milanese!
Why I remember—but I say I care not.

REG. My father, speak about thy youth. Pray tell us
What exploits thou hast done, how thou wert decked,
What sentiments of valor fired thy breast;
Let it be known to these degenerate youths
How far behind the mark of chivalry
They have receded.

JER.   No, my girl, no, no—
Some other theme must suit us.

UB.   If a theme
Is wanting, I will try what I can do.
Vitelli and myself have made a wager,
Which thou art to decide (*to Regina.*)

REG.   Not I, not I,
It is not possible that I could settle
What you could not decide—

UB. That we don't know, but we have both agreed
That each should tell some secret of himself

Before some judge whose fair discrimination
Should say whose story was the best.
    REG.   I tremble
To think that I must rule on such a question.
Is mine indeed the office to compare
The choicest secrets of two pregnant souls—
The mysteries that throng two manly breasts,
The cherished thoughts that fill two youthful hearts?
It is an office that I would decline
But that the wish to know prevents me.
    JER.   (*Aside.*) What does it mean? This all is mystery.
    VIT.   Sweet lady, noble sir, this entertainment
Which shall be found diverting, is devised
Entirely by my friend Uberto. Truly
I enter it with presage of defeat.
(*Regina seats herself, and Uberto and Vitelli prepare to tell*
    their secrets.)
    UB.   This is my tale. I wandered forth one day
Through these old woods in careless happy mood
With loving thoughts so equally bestowed,
On all I viewed that none had preference.
Sudden there came before my eyes a vision,
Which I no sooner saw than there did open
Within my heart a fount of deeper feeling
Than e'er I did suspect I could possess.
The dull placidity of former years
Seemed cold and tasteless to my new-born want,
And the sweet poignancy that struck my breast,
Was something it were bétter suffer *with*
Than to be blest without.
    REG.   And is this all?
The other story surely must be better.
    VIT. I'd fain know more. Oh! give us her description.
    UB. Her form at rest was like to some fair statue
Which the bold sculptor touched for the last time,
And feared to touch again. She moved all grace,
Her cheek was tinged with beauty's loveliest hue ;
Her eyes were darkness with light breaking through ;
The dignity she wore made praise feel weak,
And admiration stood afraid to speak.
    VIT. (*looking towards Regina.*)
Oh! rather say that hopes of such a prize
Should fire with daring even the faintest heart,
All Juno's glory shines upon her brow,
And crowns with grander lustre Venus' charms.
Heartless the man, who'd see no guardian there
To charm away all scrupulous cowardice,
Surmount all fears, all checks that might arise,
And grasp the meanest chance of such a prize.
    REG. Thou hast transcended, sir.

Ub.   Transcended me!
Jer. Good gentlemen, restrain your gaudy fancies,
Sincerity puts on no robes for show,
Which to keep new must needs be soon put off,
The garb of Truth is made for ev'ry day
And will not spoil for use—
    Vit.   My Lord, give pardon,
We come directly to the point in question.
    Reg. And thou, sir, art to tell thy secret next!
I long to hear the story of *thy* love.
    Vit. Alas! sweet lady, that this heart is free!
Freedom is dear, and yet it gives me grief
That I am not a slave—for there are slaves
Who kiss their chains and wear them as an honor,
'Twould aid me now if I were such a slave—
And yet what chance were mine against such odds?
Uberto, thou hast won—I have no secret
Which may compare in interest with thine.
Take thou the pledge—the Count need not decide;
I'll take my condemnation in advance.
(*He gives the dagger to Uberto.*)
    Ub. I'll take it without triumph over thee,
But yet in triumph.
    Reg. (*To Vitelli*)   Hast *thou* nought to say?
    Vit. Lady, I have a poor plain tale to tell,
Doomed o'er our great peninsula to wander
From court to court, studying all things I saw,
And taking part in many a fiery contest—
    Reg. Fighting for glory and the right?
    Vit.   I boast not
Of what I did nor of the light that led me,
It may be that I have followed after right,
And made a reputation. But 'tis sure
I have seen much of men, perhaps seen more
Than I have loved. And in my idleness
I have paid court to learning; many sciences—
Which men securely placed have foolishly
In well-fenced ease contemned, in toil and trouble
I have sought after. This the secret then;
That I have made acquaintance with astrology
And can reveal your fates.
    Reg. Astrology!
    Vit. Not quite decided in its faith myself,
But ready for your sakes to use the forms.
All the imposing signs.
    Reg. What forfeit, sir,
Wouldst thou have won had I decided for thee?
    Ub. I promised him a horse.
                 'Tis now too late—
    Reg. You have decided for yourselves.
    2*

Vit.   (*aside.*)   Too late!
Too late for *him*. The triumph all is mine,
Though he hath got the wager. Me she loves.
 Ub. (*To Regina*,) It shall be as thou say'st.
 Vit.   And she will say
What has been said.
 Jer. Trifles may suit our purpose when we play
But the chief end of life is serious. Let us go,
There has been too much folly.
  (*Exit, leading his daughter. Uberto follows.*)
 Vit. Why should I let my genius be outstripped
By amiable stupidity like this?
I'll play a match with thee, while I'll be winner.
Ah! I have shot a ball throughout their households
That long shall tingle. It was fate that did it.
Shall I not follow what I did not seek
But what did seek me? Yea, I'll follow it.
She shall be mine, if but for triumph—yes.
'Tis but an episode in that great volume
Which my ambition shall afford the world.

[End of First Act.]

———•—•———

ACT II.

Scene 1.—*The Garden as before.—Moonlight.—Jerome
 Forli, Uberto, Vitelli, Regina, and two Maidens discov-
 ered.—All are seated except Vitelli, who holds a Scroll in
 hand.*
 Vit. Ye glorious orbs, that seem but points of light
In the vast courses that are set for you,
Shining, with radiance and with magnitude
So much reduced, and thus so merciful
To our enquiring eyes, that we may mark
Your orbits, inconceivably immense,
Upon a little scroll—is this belief
Misplaced and vain, which calls ye Intellects
That rule the seeming chances of our world?
Or, is this doubt unworthy which denies you
A power accordant with your glorious place?
The learning of the Universities
Hath with such cold adherence to its texts
On things like this, where texts are secondary,
Rather left room for wayward speculation
Than shown firm ground for faith.
It may be that a heavenly planted instinct
Doth in a certain limit guide your ways,
That from your aspects and from your conjunctions

Proceeds a spiritual force—I wonder,
And as my wonder grows, I feel my littleness.
(*Then to his audience.*)
For you whose minds may be disposed to faith
In the predictions of astrology,
I undertake to draw your horoscopes
With skill and accuracy—though the professor
Who hesitates to vouch for the efficiency
Of what he makes his study, must at length
Lose both his time and office.
   REGINA. (*To the maidens.*)   What humility
United with what learning!
   JER.   For myself,
Signor Vitelli, I believed it once:
Once I gave credit to the "heavenly science."
Now, I believe but what's revealed and sure;
And so with all the toys that lured my youth
I rank astrology.
   VIT.   What sayest thou, fair lady?
   REG. What thy prediction tells me, I'll believe
As firm as the already finished fact
Which every eye attests. And this, my faith,
Which from assumption would gain little force,
Is strengthened by the opposite.
   VIT.   Uberto?
   UB. And I'll believe enough to make the test.
   VIT. Then we three meet at midnight in this place.
The hour is not far off. The signal, lady,
That thou art wanted, shall be this—the shadow
Of the great tower in its silent circle,
Seen from thy window in the other court,
Shall sudden die out with the sinking moon—
Then come—all others shall be at their rest.
   REG. Then I will come—both will be here?
   UB.   My duty
Is but to wait on thee.
   JER.   Then we'll retire—
And blissful dreams to those who seek their rest,
And better sense to those who study folly.
Waiting with patience for the moon to set
That so their learning may enlighten them!
And if their folly last but for a night
We give them not a malediction.
   VIT. (*To Regina*)   Watchful.
   REG. I'll be watchful.   (*Ex. Jer., Reg. and maidens.*)
   UB. We have some time to talk—thou art my friend?
   VIT. Thou sayst but truth in this—I am thy friend.
   UB. It is in this belief that I confess
What bitter days I've spent since we came hither.
I have experienced such unkindnesses

As ne'er before were shewn by her to me,
Which neither I am conscious I've deserved
Nor can suppose I have misunderstood.
To me it has been such a week of pain
As in my life before has had no pattern.
   VIT. And all this proves how deep in love thou art.
I have seen men, Uberto, so made up
Of sensitive material, that their life,
Full of fierce tenderness, shewed like malignancy.
Thou art not of that sort—thy better nature
Shews a well-balanced, well-composed humanity.
Thou art not one to look at trifles savagely
And groan without some reason—so I think—
But, sir, the toughest of us, when once pierced
By Cupid's shaft, will shrink so tremblingly
From every passing thing, that with some truth
The state of love is called the *tender* passion.
   UB. Then thou dost think that there is nothing meant
By this capricious change—now answer me :
Thou hast conversed with her so many times,
In truth, much oftener than I of late—
That thou canst judge, with a well-practised power.
   VIT. 'Tis as a navigator should return
From midst the ocean, where he sailed for years
And ask for guidance from some dusty traveller
Who never saw the sea—if thou'lt believe me—
I'm just as poor a guide in those sweet mazes.
   UB. But thou canst tell, at least, the signs of love :
   VIT. I tell thee, that in matters of the heart,
I am as dull as though I had no heart ;
But there are other bearings in this matter
On which I might give counsel—tell me first,
If thou hast asked her father for her hand ?
   UB. I have, and he displayed so good a will
To give me what I asked, yet gave it not,
That I cannot but refer his hesitation
To this unkind demeanor shown by her
Which he cares not to cross.
   VIT-   I see it now;
It is the craft of age thou hast to fear,
Not the caprice of youth—mark me, Uberto—
The lady is right beautiful.
   UB.   Alas !
   VIT. And rich.
   UB.   And rich : I'd rather she were poor.
   VIT. Her beauty and her wealth would be an ornament
Within a monarch's home :
   UB.   The worse my fate
If I should lose what monarchs might be proud of.
   VIT. It seems to me the fault is in thyself—

Ub. Perhaps it is: I am unworthy of her!

Vit. Take my advice and mend one great defect;
Men with grey hairs and daughters don't admire
That dreamy negligence thy home exhibits:
They like to dream, but 'tis on easy chairs
Where comfortable thoughts of things possessed
Can visit them—the poetry they love
Is not the self-infliction that aspires
To lofty consolations for things lost:
'Tis rather the delight in things retained
Anticipating better things to come.
The old man likes to see the young man provident,
Watching the smaller loss and gain of life
Not with his head so raised that he must grope
While looking to the sun and seven stars
To aid his good intentions.

Ub.   Sour but wholesome!
Make it more sharp; 'twill find the quicker entrance;
My ears are open.

Vit.   Put a new face on things:
Let signs of emptiness, misuse, and poverty
Be banished from thy home—then take them there;
And when they see the change, thou'lt see a change.

Ub. I'll go to-morrow and commence this work.

Vit. Now, is the word—to-night before to-morrow—
Begin the work to-night: return to-morrow.

Ub. I will: thou art a friend: give me thy hand,
My orders shall be given this very night.

Vit. Make some arrangement—stay a day, two days—
Commence thy changes with to-morrow's light:
Get up a feast with music in the hall;
Set the retainers in becoming trim—
When all's prepared, come hither suddenly;
Take them to see what is prepared for them,
Let there be pleasure well-arranged and ordered;
And let the change which ev'rywhere is felt
Proceed from a great change within thyself.

Ub. Oh! excellent.   Meantime, speak to Regina.
Let thy astrology take up my cause:
Find out her heart—and so, my good adviser,
Farewell!   (*Exit.*)

Vit.   Farewell! I *have* found out her heart.
When first she saw me, she turned cold to him,
An understanding not avowed by either
Exists between us—now the ground is clear:
And she shall fly with me this very night.
Self-accusation touched me for a moment
When now his hand met mine—come, villainy,
Drive from my heart all weak or useless thoughts!
A villain!   That's the name that some would give me,

If they could see my heart—all things are relative.
Could they but know the villains I have known,
They'd wonder at my want of imitation.
This day Uberto's nature will be changed,
He'll be a devotee in worldly practice.
I have known men thus suddenly enlightened,
Who rushed to murder.   This is needless work.—
One of that stamp *he* is, and I must watch him—
There will be condemnation for this act;
There will be execration for Vitelli.
Call it at worst a stain—my future glory
Will blot it from the dazzled eyes of men:
Or if it yet appear, they'll merely say
I was not perfect.   'Tis a charming night;
Mark how those Appennines with changeless peaks
Of chilly grandeur soar upon the view!
They give instruction to the steadfast mind:
I wish I were beyond them with my prize.
See the pale shadow with the light that made it
Steals from the sight—'tis our appointed signal.
Thus when my chequered life is at its close
The glory and the stain shall go together.

   (*Regina comes through a doorway, muffled.*)

Reg. Where is Uberto?   I don't see him here!

Vit. Sweet lady, he is here—that is to say
He has been here, and soon he will return.
But there is ample time to fix thy fate
Ere he come back.

Reg.   But tell me, is there truth
In this ambitious science, if there be,
With undissembled eagerness I ask
What are my future fates?

Vit.   ——'There's but one question
For which I read futurity's dark book.
Love is the only question of our life
For which I search the stars.

Reg.   And is not that
The chiefest source of woe or spring of joy;
Of greatest grief or deepest ecstacy?

Vit. The planets by their aspects and conjunctions
Point out the fates that wait our separate aims.
But to direct our sympathy or choice
We owe obedience only to our will,
Which is a power more sacred and supreme
Than any star that rolls.

Reg. But will is fickle, fickleness is sin;
To loathe to-morrow what we love to-day,
Is casting off allegiance to our honor.

Vit. There's an allegiance due unto *ourselves*—
If honor ask us to oppose its needs,

Then honor is both tyrannous and false.
The honor we should heed is that which tells us
To nobly follow what our hearts suggest.
   Reg. I cannot say if this bold thought be true,
I know its power to urge me—I won't listen ;
Oh! tell me, will Uberto soon be here—
I will not stay his coming.
   Vit.   Let him stay
Or let him come—this business must be followed.
Lady, thou seest before thee one whose heart
Long seeking something nobler, purer, lovelier
Than the mere crowd presents, which he might worship
To lift him o'er a world which he detests—
Nay! do not start but hear me—I will speak
   Reg. Speak then, but come not near me—then we part.
   Vit. I loved thee when I saw thee : cold till then
I felt the power which was for aye to change me ;
And with unhesitating certainty
I bowed my heart to its benignant sway !
   Reg. Oh! cease. Oh! cease! how couldst thou thus have bowed,
Thou saw'st no signs of promise, or no hope
Of happy issue to such daring confidence.
   Vit. Lady, I saw more deeply than thou thinkest.
I saw thy soaring spirit like my own—
A spirit that delights in venturous deeds,
In change of clime, in brilliant novelty,
In enterprize, which like a spring in life
Sets all its currents flowing : in long travel
Which shows us human hearts and human faces,
Social enigmas, warlike pageantries,—
A spirit which disdains a petty space,
Which can not cringe to daily, drowsy homilies —
   Reg. O truth, truth, truth! canst thou be dangerous ?
Oh! speak no more, for while thou speak'st I hear.
These words but paint my woe. They clearly shew
The desert road which I must shortly travel.
   Vit. Not so, not so ; whatever road thou walk'st
I'll follow it and cheer thee on thy way :
There are no deserts in this land of ours ;
Here all is fair and yet the fairest part
Lies off beyond the mountains where I dwell.
Oh! fly with me, fly now and be my bride.
I swear to give thee honor, love, devotion.
All the precedence woman can desire.
   Reg. Ah! no —I can not, can not go   so much restrains me —
What would Uberto say ?
   Vit.   He's but a poet :
Posterity will owe him recompense ;
And let him now take payment in advance !
Let him take up his pen, and set his wrong

To verse, and bribe the future with a song.

REG. This madness must have end—we two must part!
I will not wed Uberto, nor wed thee—
I have a father; I'll cling to him:
I'll find in duty my supreme reward.

VIT. Impossible thy fire of life would pale
Beneath such chilly and unjust restraint:
All is prepared—my friends are not far off.
        (*They go towards the side - suddenly she stops.*)

REG. Prepared, prepared, sir! Keep thy preparation
For other needs than this—I will not go—
Stand off—I'll call my father.

VIT.   Call him! Yes!
Thou canst afford to woo publicity:
There will be tongues enough about this matter,
And ev'ry tongue of them will call out shame
If thou returnest now upon thy path.
Thou hast already entered on thy journey
Five steps—thou darest not return.

REG.   O Heaven!
Father! forgive me: now thy words return
Unto my memory with tenfold force.

VIT. I say, Uberto momently may come,
And I unarmed - the fool has won my dagger.
I can bring here one hundred valiant arms
And carry off the household by a beck.
Ho! there, my trusty servants, you are wanted.

[*From one side appear the two retainers who appeared in the
    first scene, and in a moment after from the other side, ap-
    pears Matteo Arcano. The first two take charge of the lady
    who is half irresolute, while Vitelli confronts Arcano.*]

ARCANO. I come to seek my lord. So many days
He has been absent, and such evil dreams
Have troubled me, I wish to solve my doubts.

VIT. He has gone home, and passed thee on the road.

ARC. But why are ye asunder? What has happened?
And is not this the lady of the castle
That seems in durance? I'll not be responsible,
But summon all the household—

VIT.   Thou hast risked
The heaviest responsibility
Thy life has e'er presented. See to him.

[*Vitelli relieves his servants of charge of the lady, and they
    approach Arcano. Each stabs him in turn.*]

1ST RETAINER. Thou need'st not answer them, if they should ask.

2ND RET. Thy stewardship is over.

(*Regina turns her head and sees the deed, and as they bear
    her off, she cries "Villains, Villains!"*)

ARC. I die a faithful steward. [*Dies.*]

        (*A few moments elapse, and enter Uberto.*)

Ub. The day advances—they have left the court.
Strange travelling has been mine throughout the night—
I did not think when leaving, my return
Should be so instant. My old faithful steward
Urged by strange fears –so 'twas explained to me --
Had hastily come hither. That is strange :
It was good counsel that Vitelli gave me,
And badly hindered. *(Enter Jerome Forli.)*
     Here is Jerome Forli
Abroad so soon, what shall I say to him ?
  Jer. Uberto !
  Ub.   Aye, my lord.
  Jer. And here alone !
  Ub.   Alone. But—but, thou art disturbed.
  Jer. I *am* disturbed to find thee here alone.
  Ub. That's easily explained –but has aught happened
To call thee thus so early from thy rest ?
  Jer. Nothing. I slept contentedly and sound,
Till nearly at the first grey light of dawn,
I thought I heard some faint but startling sound
Here in the court –and here alone I find thee.
Explain, sir.
  Ub. I cannot explain, my lord.
I found the court all silent. I have come
To seek my servant.
  Jer.   Thou hast come to seek thy servant!
But that thy character is known to me—
Tell me where are my daughter and Vitelli ?
I left you three together. Tell me—tell me
Where are my daughter and Vitelli ?
  Ub. I know not. I have been at home –
  Jer.   At home ?
By his persuasion ?
  Ub.   'Twas by his persuasion.
  Jer. Then while thou wert at home, the devil was here,
And he has triumphed. *(Falls on a seat.)*
  Ub. I don't understand.
  Jer. *(rising).* Don't understand ! Thou hast no understanding.
Here, Giacomo –call the maidens –here.
        (Enter servant, maidens and others).
Stir up the varlets from their beds. Go thou   *(To Giacomo.)*
Unto Vitelli's chamber. Say he's wanted.
Go ye and tell your lady to come hither.   *(To the maidens.)*
    (Uberto discovers the body of Matteo Arcano.)
  Ub. What ! My servant whom I sought lies murdered here !
  Jer. Arcano murdered !
  Ub. He came to seek me while I sought for him
Two reeking stabs !
  Jer. It is Vitelli's work.

3

Ub. Ah! surely no —my poor old servant murdered!
(*Kneeling*) And how hast thou deserved it, my poor servant?
Who were they that did pierce this faithful breast?
Jer.   Uberto, listen.
    (*Servants re-enter.*)
Giacomo. Signor Vitelli is not in the castle.
Maidens. Our mistress is not found—
Jer.   Depart at once.
Stir every living soul within the walls.
Uberto. listen. Hast thou sense or hearing?
  Ub. My poor dead servant!
  Jer. (*To the men-servants, who are going.*)
Cart that dead ass out of the court. (*They take the body.*)
                      Uberto.
  Ub. What dost thou mean?
  Jer.   Thou art as guilty,
As tainted with confederacy with him,
As if with open-eyed, cold-hearted malice,
Thou had'st designed this deed.
    Ub.   What deed, my lord?
  Jer. Is not their guilt as plain and palpable
As it shall be when they are hither brought,
With a cold dagger in each wanton heart?
  Ub. My lord, I don't believe.
  Jer.   And when wilt thou?
My daughter and Vitelli both have fled,
And thou that daughter's lover, standest here
In double-drenched stupidity, which only
That I am meek and changed from what I was,
Would at my hands as proof of guilty knowledge,
Deserve a halter.
    Ub.   'Tis impossible. (*Exit.*)
    Jer.   Bring my armor
You useless, loitering, meek-faced hypocrites.
(*Two servants bring a breast-piece which he throws away.*)
Not that - I said bring weapons, fiery weapons;
The time is come when iron for protection
Is a mere eggshell go, prepare my horse (*Ex. servants.*)
Wretched I am that cannot call around me
A hundred swearers —ere the close of day
Vitelli's carcase, on yon thick-ribbed oak
Would be suspended as a warning-post
To all such reprobates   (*Enter Uberto.*)
    Ub.   I am convinced.
  Jer. Ha! ha! Thou art convinced
Though unsuspicious, dull, half-witted —
    Ub.   True!
I *have* been dull, half-witted, unsuspicious,
Incredulous of evil—I am changed:

I will amend that error of the heart.

JER. Then haste, Oh! haste, thou art at length convinced
Oh! bring me back my daughter, good Uberto.

UB. Let them pursue to whom pursuit brings comfort!
Thou mayest bring back a daughter by pursuit ;
If *I* pursue, what thing do I bring back?

JER. Inexplicable man, and canst thou reason
At such a time so coldly ?   If the lover
Can know no touch of anger, can the friend
Not feel one generous throb of sympathy
For age dishonored, for a noble house
Disgraced ?

UB.   I once was generous – henceforth
I look alone to my own cause and honor.
Uberto is not one to hunt up truants.
He makes no exhibition of his griefs
For the amusement of the sneering world.

JER. Then thou, the last hope of my waning life,
Thou hast deceived me.   I myself will go,
And though no spark of feeling animates thee,
I give thee not my curse.   If I come back,
And bring not back my daughter, then I pray
That never human face may comfort me ;
That this old home be blasted from the earth !
Let there be but a grave on yonder slope.—
It is the only place where then
My daughter will not trouble me –farewell !   (*Exit.*)

UB. Farewell !   Deceived, dishonored, slighted, trampled !
I'll think of them no more.   My love for her
Is dead.   There's beauty in the serpent's skin,
And what more beauteous than the tiger's spots,—
But therefore, shall we foolishly adore
Venom or treachery ? I'm safe from this.
He, he, the subtle, plotting, smiling, villain.—
Can I, with mere indifference think of him ?
No, no, by all that's just, henceforth I swear
To be his evil genius – I will track him
Through all the ends of earth.   Away with virtue ;
Fair play and honor – when we track a wolf,
These are not words the hunter cares to think of.
I'll go abroad with malice in my heart
And be prepared to meet the worst of them—
They're all Vitelli's friends—but he nor they
Shall find me e'er again what once I was.

(*Bellamori looks through the window of a ruin.*)
BELLAMORI. Here is a captain will assist thy purpose.
UB. Bellamori ! (*Bellamori comes forward.*)
BELL. I know what has occurred.   Say not a word.
UB. O Bellamori, say thou canst forgive me !
BELL. I can, I will—my old fidelity

Did not desert me when I left your castle.
Finding my legs were free, I cast about me
To find some of our Free Companions— gentlemen
Whose time was on their hands and who desired
A certain special sort of work to do—
In short I pitied you. I thought I'd offer
One chance to rub away the rust of peace.
The men are here, and they shall call you captain,
If you but speak the word.
    Ub. O Bellamori,
The world stands half-redeemed, while I can clasp thee
It is the timeliness of kindly aid
Which grief appreciates.
    Bell. The men are waiting—
Say you will be their captain.
    Ub. Bellamori,
I want them to be executioners
Upon Vitelli. No! 'Tis I myself—
If ever when a fair occasion offers,
I shall be found so cold, so ill-advised,
So occupied with intervening accidents
Which time may yet throw forward to delude me,
As to reprieve the twentieth of a minute
That felon heart of his.—But dost thou know it?
    Bell. I heard the tale this morning. This upset
Was needed to remove the curse of peace
That lay upon you. Had I been in time
To stop Vitelli, all would have been spoiled;
My best desires for thee were all in vain,
And this enchanting object which of late
So often drew your feet to Forli's castle,
Would have remained a sweet incumbrance still,
Instead of kindly taking wings. Hold! hold!
You surely do not think to strike a man
That brings you such a band.
    Ub. Good Bellamori,
Wilt thou give me thy honor as a soldier,
That thou wilt execute upon Vitelli
The vengeance he has earned—provided first,
That the precedence in the work of justice
Be given to me? Do you engage me this?
    Bell. I do.
    Ub. Give me thy hand.
    Bell. It is arranged.
And now our chiefest business is with glory –
Plunder and glory. Forward, soldiers.
    (*Enter a band of Free Companions.*)
Soldiers, behold your leader! I am now
But one among you; look to him in future!
Henceforth regard thyself a man! Till now

I looked upon you merely as a baby ;
A baby born in an unwholesome place
Where the plague—the plague of peace —was deadly.
Now you've outgrown your doll, you please me better,
Ah! the hand upon the dagger —a nice one too —
Faith you're a captain 'twill be hard to play with!
Now I'm obedience. (*He takes his place in rank.*)
   Ub. Keep in mind your promise !
   Bell. Hail our captain !
   Soldiers. Hail our noble captain ! (*Cheering.*)
   Ub. Lead the way.

[End of Second Act.]

ACT III.

Scene 1. *An Inn in Savoy.— Uberto, Bellamori, and a band of Free Companions sitting or reclining.*

SONG.

Take heed, take heed, ye burghers !
  Your wealth is in our hands :
Your fortresses can not avail
  To check our marching bands.
But if ye would be happy,
  Then welcome us with cheers ;
And bring your purses to your gates,
  And hang them on our spears.

     Chorus.—For we are Free Companions,
       And roving Cavaliers.
       The echoing land is all awake,
       To view our glancing spears.

Take heed, take heed, ye princes !
  Your thrones are in our way ;
To prop them up or fling them down,
  Must be as we shall say.
But if ye would be happy,
  Or if your pains would cease,
Then fling your cares into our cups,
  And ye may sleep in peace.
              Chorus.

Take heed, take heed, ye nations !
  Take heed, take heed, ye powers !
Our lances all are in your lines,
  Your rights may all be ours.
But if ye would be happy,
  Or would your breasts be free,
Then leave your cause within our camps,
  And take whate'er shall be.
              Chorus.

8*

UBERTO. Soldiers! we have fought two years together;
And in pursuit of further fields of fame
I've led you unto Charles, Duke of Savoy
And King of Cyprus, who will shortly lead
An expedition into fair Provence.
Here we will rest, until with freshened vigor
We may pursue our journey to Turin.

(To Bellamori.)

Thou pattern of Free Lances, watch for all;
And speak not with the people of the inn.

BELL. Warily, warily, good Captain! I never saw a young man of his years improve so fast. This love is a thing that I hope will never bother me. Here is, we will say, a serviceable man, every way good for war—all of a sudden he sees a face in a wood, and from that day he is the follower of that face; he loses his senses for sake of that face, and one fine day when a friend comes round and steals the pretty picture, then he is roused to energy, but still on account of that face. Now may the infected atmosphere of peace engulf me for ever and ever, if I would consent to be fooled in this way. Never shall any picture painted on flesh or canvass make Bellamori such a traitor to himself. *(Enter Bonita and Pietro.)* What, what do I feel? Delilah must be come to town and no doubt with a whole pack of treachery in her head. This is the suddenest turn I ever experienced. I should not wonder if I would be cutting people's throats by and by for the sake of this little eater of chesnuts.

BONITA. Illustrious sir.

BELL. Good! that deserves a hearing.

BONITA. May it please you, we are poor Savoyards who keep this inn; and my father, who, you may see, is very much afraid—

PIETRO. No, no! don't say that. I am not afraid.

BON. Well, my father and I—or I, for my father is so much afraid—thought if you wouldn't be good enough to just rise up and go away and never let us see any of you again. Such a handsome soldier as you, I know, will take pity on me, and go away just as soon as ever you can.

BELL. What is your name—instantly?

BON. Bonita, sir; just Bonita.

BELL. And you are her father?

PI. Yes, sir. I am Pietro, her father.

BELL. Bonita I love you.

BON. and PI. Oh! *(And they retire.)*

UB. What is the matter, Bellamori?

BELL. The people of the inn were speaking in their sleep.

UB. Stretch your halberd through two crotchets of an oak. Sling a stout rope thereon. Call yourself provost-marshal. Summon them up and shew it to them. Tell them that people in war time have no right to talk through their sleep.

BELL. Very good –well, suppose all that done.

(*Re-enter Bonita and Pietro, with a large pitcher.*)

BON. Most valiant sir!

PI. And well-favored! Say well-favored –

BON. And well-favored! We have returned through the excess of our fear.

BELL. Good! I like to strike fear.

BON. There comes here sometimes one Marco Tracco,—and some others, too—and Marco Tracco chiefly says, that if any one but himself says he loves me, he will cut his nose off.

BELL. Does he wear a sword?

BON. and PI. Marco Tracco wear a sword!

BON. If he wore a sword, sir, my father would not listen to him for a moment.

BELL. Psha! And you?

BON. Indeed, sir, I tremble at men that have swords.

BELL. Right—right. Tell Marco Tracco to put on a sword, so that your father will not listen to him, and I may slice him. I have fought for the last two years in the hottest Italian fields.

BON and PI. Oh! dreadful.

BELL. I have been in the battle of Malignano. Florence remembers me, I promise you. You want such a man. I am one of the Free Lances. Chivalry lives with us, and dies with us. I can give you both more blows on the crown of the head than the Constable of France.

BON. (*Weeping.*) Oh! sir—spare us!

PI. We don't wish any blows on the crown of the head.

BELL. What disturbs you? Are you not satisfied?

BON. (*Still weeping.*) It is so dreadful to get married to a robber.

PI. Now we are ruined. (*He brings the pitcher.*)

BELL. What is that?

PI. My daughter would like to know if you would object to a draught of Naples wine.

BELL. I would, if it were in small quantity.

BON. We have forgot the goblet.

BELL. When I am replenished, get a goblet and measure what is left. (*He drinks it all.*)

Bonita, did I say I loved you?

BON. Illustrious sir, you said so.

BELL. And I think you said I was a robber?

BON. Yes, sir—but you could repent before we were married.

BELL. There is room for much caution in affairs like this.

UB. (*Awaking.*) Ho! Bellamori. Seize all in the house!

BELL. Go, go—I have been incautious.

BON. But, valiant sir, what becomes of the marriage?

PI. Aye—what becomes of the marriage?

BELL. I'll marry when I'm fifty if there's peace.

(*Exeunt Pietro and Bonita.*) (*The others sleep again.*)

BELL. This is a case for circumspection. I like not Marco
Tracco. (*Re-enter Bonita.*)

BON. Illustrious sir, as you love me—listen to what I have to
say. Two signors had a private interview in this room a week
ago, and they are to come to-night again. If you and your party
remain quiet and say nothing, it will all be well.

BELL. One of these is Marco Tracco ?

BON. As I hope for happiness, no—

BELL. Then describe them.

BON. The principal one is not very tall and not very strong.
He looks handsome sometimes; and when he does *not* look handsome, it is because of some expression in his dark eye, like—

BELL. Like what?

BON. Like—badness. Withal, I think he is one of the most
winning persons I ever saw, and yet I don't like him. The other—

BELL. Never mind the other. I'll do what you ask.

BON. Thanks, gentle sir.

BELL. Now, good Bonita, forget what I have said and forget
me. Retire to thy bed and sleep soundly ; I shall be in Turin ere
you awake.

BON. (*Weeping.*) 'Tis a hard sentence, if it must be. Good-bye.
(*Exit.*)

BELL. I did not think we would find Vitelli in this part of the
world—and in our very lair too. Well, the promise I made Uberto
has to be kept. So in any case we are to have a dead man. (*He
lays himself down.*) It is perfectly plain that can not be
avoided.

(*The lights are darkened and enter Vitelli and a stranger,
muffled.*)

VITELLI. This place is full of sleeping men. No matter
There is no need for words.

(*Each takes a paper from his breast ; and they exchange.*)

BELL. Arise, Uberto !—behold thy enemy ! behold Vitelli !

(*Uberto and the soldiers start up.—The stranger throws his
arms round Vitelli.*)

UB. Vitelli, thou art granted to my yearnings.

VIT. I am to die?

UB. That's certain.

VIT.   One request !
Grant me a moment to collect my thoughts.

UB. This is but fair. Remove him, Bellamori.
(*Bellamori removes the stranger.*)

VIT. If to be slain surrounded and unarmed—
If this be judgment on the life of one
Whose sins outweigh his virtues,
Then no complaint becomes me. Let me die !
I know indeed that when my heart is still,
That after thoughts based upon after knowledge,
Will vehemently wish that yet I lived
To offer nobler, fairer means of vengeance

Than are presented by assassination.

Ub. Vitelli, time is pressing. I have sworn it—

Vit. If thou canst do *that* thou hast sworn, thy name
Is not Uberto. Thou hast undertaken
A business far beneath thee—aye, as far
As is the earth from heaven. There is a vengeance—
A vengeance that will bring no stain to thee
While I am punished. Wherefore take the worst,
While the best means are equally at hand?

Ub. What means?

Vit.   By battle, equally and fair.
Art thou so niggard of thy life, so watchful
Of thy mere selfish safety, as refuse
An equal venture?

Ub. Heaven knows I am not.

Vit. And what says Bellamori? Shall the world
Have leave to say that for some dross or trinkets
On this poor body—not for old offence
In by-gone years—his dagger sought my life?

Bell. His injury is mine—

Vit.   And is not less.
I feel that I am safe. Ye are not capable
Of such a deed as would embalm the victim
In the preserving sympathy of men,
While the foul actors with successful ease
Had damned their hopes, their hearts, their future peace,
And lost their soldierly renown for ever.

Ub. The devil can tell truth when it will serve him.
                    (*Sheathes his dagger*).

[*Vitelli gradually moves backward amongst the soldiers
and towards the side entrance.*]

Vit. I can be found to-morrow, any day—
And with a sword that may have some poor skill
To further its bad cause. Good evening, sirs!
When you go back to Naples, think of me—
Guard your fair dames! Protect your ruined bulwarks.
        (*Uberto rushes between him and the door.*)

Ub. Thou hast deserved thy death again. What folly
To think of honor! Slay him, Bellamori!
(*While they rush on him, Vitelli takes out a purse which he
holds up amongst the soldiers.*)

Vit. Ye are not bound to this, Free Lances. Save me!
I am a general of Savoy. Protect me!

Soldiers. Save him! Save him!
(*They form a guard round Vitelli.— Vitelli opens his cloak
and draws a sword.*)

Vit. Now for the meaner weapon. Against odds
A sword is nothing, if it be not charmed.
Now, gentlemen, if you have prayers to say—

Soldiers. No, no we are not bound to this.

Vit.   And, therefore,
They may thank fate that their assassin thoughts
Bring them no deeper trouble.   Guard us, soldiers!
My influence with the duke will square these matters,
And even with these disappointed friends
Will act with kindness.   Don't forget Vitelli.
    (*Exeunt Vitelli, soldiers, and stranger.*)
  Ub. We are but foiled assassins.   Let them go!
The Duke expects me.   We shall meet to-morrow.
Await me in the Plaza del Castello.   (*Exit.*)
  Bell. Bonita! here!   Come hither, dear Bonita!
What is thy father's name?   Perhaps they're fled,
And all this matter will be noised about.
Vitelli has escaped; Bonita fled;
Our soldiers have deserted.   War!   War!   War!   (*Exit.*)

Scene 2.—*A hall in the Ducal Palace of Savoy.—Enter
  Regina and Bonita.*
  Reg. Girl, thy tale is strange.   But cease thy weeping.
Are all these facts exactly as thou say'st?
  Bon. I have spoke truly, madam, as I've seen;
Though I was never in Turin before
I thought it but my duty to come hither,
And tell thee of the danger that beset
The General Vitelli and the stranger.
And Marco Tracco too who loved me so—
He never could have murdered any one.
  Reg. Thou say'st that General Vitelli came
Before with this same stranger?
  Bon.   Madam—yes.
I recognised them well.   Oh! save them, lady!
But now it is too late – and in our house!
  Reg. Now go, good child—remain where I have told thee,
And listen well, the caution I now give thee!
Speak not to any one about this matter.   (*Exit Bonita.*)
Am I a woman and remain so cold,
So dull, unmoved at the report of blood,
When he, for whom I left my home, my father—
When he, who after my rash trust in him
Made me his wife and gave me dignity—
When he this day perhaps lies murdered?
I wonder at myself   I cannot grieve;
But, even at this hour, instead of tears
The strong conviction of a doom deserved
Is all the off'ring I can pay to him.
Who is this stranger that he met so secret?
Ah! there's a thought comes flashing through my brain,
That some base treachery against the duke
Was hatched between them.   If he has been murdered,
There will be time enough to weep to-morrow;

But if he lives, then, do I live to thwart him.
Uberto, too, unpractical, romantic,
Turning to vengeance all his first pure thoughts,
Comes hither.   If he missed his blow last night,
'Tis the last blow Vitelli's craft allows him
Ever to level at his breast.
Enter Vitelli.)
Thank Heaven!
VIT. What means this round-eyed wonder—this amaze ?
This mixture of the horror which is felt
When spectres show themselves, with the quick welcome,
Although a welcome perhaps coldly felt
When absent ones return.   I am Vitelli ;
And ev'rything I wot of goes on well
In this good world.
    REG.   Heav'n grant it go on well !
    VIT. Sweet wife, I am a man of many cares ;
And all these cares sit easily on me,
Whom fate has doomed to bear them – while for thee,
To whom they are not offered, all the burthen,
Anxiety and anguish seem committed.
Go, go – the duke comes hither with his court.
Join in the train- speak with the good Francesca,
The angel of the court ; I know thou'rt good,
Be also godly !
    REG.   God looks down on us ;
And in His knowledge we are both embraced.   (*Exit Regina.*)
    VIT. One only grave mistake I've made in life,
And that's my marriage.
A love of useless triumph is my bane—
Henceforth I look to solid profits only.   (*Takes out a paper.*)
I've had a keen encounter with grim death ;
He glared into my very eyes ; my heart
Began to feel that awe which dignitaries
Impose on those beneath them.   It is hard
That two mistaken men should hamper me,
And hinder my designs.   (*Looking at the paper.*)
Within a week
I shall be duke. " *Faucigny and Chablais,*"
And so forth— these are my reward,
As promised by his Majesty of France.
Meantime *they must be seen to.*   I'll make up
A statement of this case before the duke,
Which will relieve me.   Then my course is free.
And hear me, Heaven ! on whom I never call,
I will be good when I have grown thus great !
(*Enter guards with a banner, then the Duke of Savoy, with
   Uberto and Chancellor Mancini, Francesca Mancini and
   Regina.*)
DUKE. Savoy in patient strength still sits on high,

And holds the balance on her mountain tops,
To weigh the contests which arise beneath—
And now the time presents her chance for power:
   Vit. " *When Italy becomes our artichoke,*
We'll pluck it leaf by leaf."
   Duke.   A prophecy
Which could not come but from a soul that's true.
Vitelli, thou shalt stay to guard our Alps,
While this good soldier, who has come from Florence,
With our own banner marches to Provence.
             (*Uberto and Vitelli bow.*)
   Ub. (*Aside*) I see them both—now where is my revenge ?
   Duke. Sweet ladies, who thus grace our humble home,
Vitelli's noble partner—good Francesca,
Mancini's daughter, angel of our court,—
I pray let not your smiles be sadly dimmed
Because we toil abroad in war.
Let us depart unto our several tasks !
   Vit. One word, my lord : this noble Florentine –
   Ub. Not Florentine, but Neapolitan.
   Duke. Vitelli, speak. What wouldst thou say of him ?
   Reg. (*In Vitelli's ear.*) Traitor, beware !
   Vit. If he should lead Free Lances, let him watch them ;
They may go over to the enemy.
   Ub. Even so ; our enemy at first or last.
Must be prostrated.
   Duke.   We'll take care of that.
(*Exeunt guards, Duke, Uberto, Chancellor Mancini. Fran-*
cesca going out with her father returns.)
   Francesca. This is Uberto thou hast told me of ?
   Reg. 'Tis he.
   Fr.   Take care –take care ! (*Exit Francesca.*)
   Vit. Has Forli's daughter heard the news from home ?
   Reg. My father –is he dead ?
   Vit.   I am not certain.
In truth I know just nothing : I will ask—
   Reg. But who can tell us ?
   Vit.   Who ! None but Uberto.
   Reg. He scarce comes here with much good-will to us.
   Vit. I humbly ope my mind unto that knowledge.
The case stands thus. He comes - we'll say - to slay me.
Further - I'm at his feet –he stands above me.
At that dread hour I meekly look to him,
And say, "Before I pay the debt that's due thee,
Hear my request. There's an afflicted lady,
Who, greatly dreading to outlive her father,
Devoutly wishes to survive her husband ;
Longing to die, and longing more to live—
Made up of opposites, and as must follow,
So much distracted, even now I pity her—

Go be her comforter; restore her happiness:
Tell her that death has waited on her wishes
In sparing and in slaying"—
    REG.   Insolent!
There's always some such end to thy beginnings.
    VIT. Indeed, that end just now I hinted at
Would be in keeping with the harmless system
Which my whole life shall strongly illustrate.
None can deny me this! And thou, good partner,
Say, has not kindness marked my course to thee?
    REG. Thine is a sort of kindness which at first
Cheers like the radiance coming from the hearth—
But ere the favored one can feel its glow,
It turns into the spare and glimmering torch
Of the incendiary.
    VIT. And yet my motives are above exception.
Many there are who can not understand me.
    REG. And they must suffer?
    VIT. They obstruct my way.
    REG. And what of those who seek thee through intention
To punish or to check thee?
    VIT.   Like Uberto?
If with pure pity for his childishness
I could remove him without injury,
That would be economical of trouble.
But there are cases which require some trouble.
A word of explanation to the duke
Shall take him from my trail.
    REG.   I pray refrain:
Say nothing to the duke.
    VIT.   And say, why not?
    REG. Heed an unhappy woman's stern command:
Say nothing to the duke!
    VIT.   And why unhappy?
Have I not kept all promises with thee,
I made that night now nearly two years past,
When we took candid counsel with each other,
And left thy father's house? Have I not made thee
My honored wife, the equal of myself?
    REG. A woman's honor rests in her own hands,
Few others care to guard it—thou the last.
I know what thou wouldst do if thou didst dare—
A woman's honor needs her own protection,
Or else not bars, not bolts, not vigilance,
Nor jealous guardianship, nor staid respect,
Can save her from the gulf.
    VIT.   Then I must thank thee
For the kind confidence that trusted in me.
    REG. Because I e'er was wilful, never weak;
Because I could enforce at dagger's point
    4

The terms I made, ev'n wert thou lord of earth,
And couldst engulf me in its lowest mine.

VIT. But this is needless; all that's claimed is granted:
Thou art we'll say, a very virtuous wife—
Very didactic, most exemplary.
Have I not granted thee all privilege,
Ease, dignity, adornment of a wife?
Have I not been a husband kind to thee?

REG. As good a one as a bad man can be.
I had a dream, while dreaming was my wont,
Of such a husband as would please my heart—
One able to keep credit amongst men,
Able to match the worst and please the best;
Potent but gracious wise but not deceitful.
That night of error so entranced my eyes,
I thought I found him – soon the colder light
Informed me of the baseness which usurped
So chivalrous a bearing.

VIT.   I too erred
In due appreciation of thy merits:
Thou canst paint portraits—

REG.   And they have a truth
To make thee wince if thou dost know thyself.

VIT. Thy hand is rash at coloring.   Take care!

REG. Sneering at all that's noble in this life;
Mocking at truth; turning thy back on love;
Scouting at honor; honoring but *self*,
And using all the means which *self* may counsel;
Craft, if 'twill serve, if not, then cruelty;
Deceiving all at first, and no one long;
Where'er thou art there treachery springs up—
And thou canst flourish there till indignation
Chase thee away.

VIT. O flattery, I've found thy opposite!
A wife is but a double-visaged Janus;
For the first quarter she sheds peace upon you;
But war is in reserve.

REG. All this fair-seeming confidence thou wearest
Is but the impudence of long success.

VIT. Ah, but I have one virtue which outstrips
All these great vices--I have wondrous patience;
But I may lose it, too.   Take care!   Take care!

REG. I do not try thy patience—mine is tried,
Te see thee as thou art.

VIT.   Whate'er I am,
Accursed or blessed, I've not done wrong to thee.
Men have two spheres, but women only one;
Whate'er we do abroad concerns us only.
The husband not the man should be thy study;
Finding the husband faultless, 'tis unwise,

Presumptuous to criticise the man.
I'll guard my safety as a man should do ;
And when I guard my safety, I guard thine :
Taunt me no more—I'll do what I designed.

REG. I will not taunt, but threaten : do it not !

VIT. I understand thee—thou wouldst spare Uberto ?

REG. I care not for Uberto—if I did
I had not been to-day the wretch I am.

VIT. If this be not the motive, wherefore then
Refuse to have this matter fully stated
Before the duke, and the assassin checked ?

REG. Shall I avow my reason ?

VIT.   State it boldly,
Since boldness is thy wont.

REG.   'Tis not my wish
That men should know the foul infatuation
Which thralled my heart when I made choice of thee.

VIT. And what if I make known this ill-starred choice ?

REG. Then *I* make known a bitter fact for thee !

VIT. What is that fact ?

REG.   'Tis treason to the duke—
I've marked those secret messages and letters,
Those words which in the idiotcy of treason
Conspirators let fall—ha, ha, I've guessed it ;
Thou meanest to let the French upon the Alps
When the duke's army is engaged beyond.
Ah ! now I see thy coldness can take fire.

VIT. When it takes fire, that day thou art consumed.
                      (*Seizing her by the wrist.*)
If thou dost breathe this thought, thou breath'st no more ;
I will not vent my rage on thee in words ;
But sure as death or vengeance, if a nod,
A glance, a smile, should hint at this suspicion,
My hand shall stifle all thy biting taunts—
Sure as the adamantine gates of death ;
The hungry plague ; the sweeping scythe of war ;
The unrelenting tiger's bounding rage ;
The all-annihilating stroke of power
With which the roused leviathan assails
When puny hands in his cold home molest him—
That tongue now venturing upon things outside thee
Shall have reviled thy executioner.

REG. Wouldst murder me !

VIT.   Aye – I will murder thee :
And I will tell what tomb shall open for thee—
In the dumb darkness of the hideous night,
Helpless within the circling power of him
Whom thou hast maddened by thy wilfulness,
Out of thy home, unto those awful wilds,
Where quiet souls ne'er come, thou shalt be hurried !

In some deep gorge to hunter's only known,
Thy body shall be flung—and as thy spirit
Would ever sit upon some lofty height,
The Alps shall be thy monument—remember.
Now to my home, to see what must be done.   (*Exit.*)

REG. My father, O my father, thy displeasure
Aided by retribution's hand, pursues me.
Dearer to me one silver hair of thine
Than all the selfish flatteries of men!
The good Francesca, who knows all my story,
She who has words of comfort on her lips,
And loving pardon in her heart, comes hither.
                    (*Enter Francesca.*)
FRA. This is Uberto, thou has told me of?
REG. This is the man to whom, next to my parent,
I've offered most respect and most contempt.
FRA. There is a pale abstraction on his brow
Which rather shows a rancor felt with pain
Than gloating exultation of revenge.
Uberto must be seen and reasoned with:
The duke's authority may be called forth.
REG. Nay, nay—tell not the duke! let justice triumph!
Uberto seeks revenge; let him attain it!
Vitelli ne'er will die a nobler way
Than this presents him—I am tired of life
But yet Uberto hath no kind of right
To take my life.   I used a woman's freedom
To give my hand where my own wishes pointed,
I was not wed to him; I had the power
If so I chose, to blast my future life;
And now my life, though blasted, is my own.
FRA. There's one consideration thou forgett'st
Attaching to this question of revenge.
These murders that we dread, which far outweighs
Vitelli's life and thine.
REG.   And what is that?
FRA. It is the crime committed against heaven.
REG. Thy aim is always still too high for me.
FRA. I will not sleep secure and see such deeds,
No matter how provoked, brought to their issue,
Nor make such efforts as one poor weak hand
May timely try to check them ere they rise.
REG. Thou canst do nothing but inform the duke—
And that shall not be done.
FRA.   I can do much.
Believe me, while engaged in the duke's service
He will make truce with his revengeful thoughts;
But peace restored, he will resume his object
When loyalty will not obstruct his way.
REG. Then that gives hope unto thy saintly spirit.

That crime may be prevented. I'll be calm,
And make my hopes like thine, though Heav'n can see
How far I am from being like to thee.   (*Exeunt.*)
SCENE 3. - *The Plaza del Castello—a deep doorway in the
centre with a window overhead—enter Bellamori with a
halberd.*

BELLAMORI. This, they tell me, is the Plaza del Castello ; and
this building is the house of the Chancellor that has the saintly
daughter. If her ladyship knew I was so near she would be
visited with a fit of the chills. She, too, of course, cannot endure
a *robber.* I wonder what she thinks of this great robbing expedition into Provence. Ah ! Bonita, Bonita, my first love, why is
it that I must give thee up ? The case summed up is simply this—
that a wife in time of war is no more or less than an enemy in the
rear, eating up a man's provisions. Now may the rust of peace
consume me, and a bottomless stagnation of peace circumfuse me,
and may I never more look upon a field of spoil, but here comes
Bonita herself with that ancient incumbrance she calls her father.
Now they may have come hither to report the little affair of the
inn ; therefore, it may be better not to meet them until I hear
something from Uberto. Ah ! here is one of your grand vestibules,
under where the saint resides. I wonder if she knows by instinct
what an amount of sin now enters here.

(*He hides in the doorway - enter Bonita and Pietro.*)

PI. The signor is not dead ?

BON. He is not dead. I saw him with my own eyes. I suppose
he paid them a ransom and they let him go. But for that matter,
they are all rogues together.

PI. Oh ! hush - hush. What fine houses ?

BON. Beautiful houses ! It is only quiet people like you and
me that are poor.

PI. Now daughter, the soldier said he loved thee. I know our
duke by reputation ; he will make him keep his word. What a
fine thing his helmet would be if we hung it up to hold salt.

BON. Nay, father, it is your thought. He has a robbing look
about him that frightens me, while poor Marco Tracco is so gentle.

BELL. (*Aside.*) Marco Tracco !

BON. But, as we are in the city, I would like to see him well
enough. As for going to the duke, I have been in the palace
already, and it did not frighten me so very much.

PI. Oh ! I don't know what to say. I am afraid we will never
get back safe to our little inn. Why did you bring me here at all ?
Oh ! look, look, look !

(*Enter Vitelli - Pietro and Bonita fall on their knees and
cry.*)

BON. O amiable and well-favored signor, forgive us ; we had
nothing whatever to do with your murder.

PI. Nor with the murder of the beautiful muffled gentleman
that came along with you.

VIT. Now, is the arch-fiend so busy with my interests
4*

That he can leave the wide deserving world,
To weave his plots for me.   Old man, has age
So left you freedom of your limbs, you venture
So rashly into danger of your neck?
Young girl, thou dost not know the plague of camps.
Away—there will be seventeen hundred lances here,
And each a born-devil, with martial law
To back their pranks and turn their outrages
All into virtues to be recompensed—
And all within five minutes.
    (*Bonita and Pietro cry, and hastily retire.*)
Am I indeed secure, when at each moment
These incidents, like signs that to the mariner
Reveal his danger, come to warn me—ha! (*Enter Uberto*).
 UB. Pass on thou hateful villain! tempt me not!
 VIT. Pointed, yet vague—my name, Sir, is Vitelli.
 UB. 'Tis shorter to say 'villain' than 'Vitelli.'
 VIT. Thou hast a mind to stab me as I pass?
 UB. Had I the mind, the deed ere now were done.
 VIT. Why dost thou wear that dagger but for me?
  (*Francesca looks cautiously through the window.*)
 UB. I reason but with men; wolves I pass by,
Till the fit time arrives to slaughter them.
 VIT. It seems the wolf may live a little while.
(*He crosses in his first direction ; Francesca shows joy at
 the window.*)
Now this is candid; this is timely warning;
I find that thou hast yet a noble soul:
There are some men who once and only once
Have made a true profession of themselves;
But finding things go wrong in consequence,
Turned them to wiser things—others can ne'er
Keep back the true pronouncement—'tis unwise:
I would not wish a friend to be so open.
 UB. Though I have pledged my word, thou art not safe.
 VIT. Oh! thou wilt keep to word and candor both.
I courted candor once, sweet smiling dame—
The courtship proved indeed but very short,
For she betrayed me—then I gave respect
Unto her step-sister, a cunning lady
Who wears an ugly likeness to herself—
So I and candor have been since at war.
 UB. Fiend! hold thy peace, or I will maim thy tongue
And send thee face to face with all the fiends
To mispronounce thy mockery—away!
 VIT.   One question more—where is our Bellamori?
If he's not with thee, then I'm safe indeed:
Thou wouldst not wield a dagger, but our captain
Would plunge his knife into his father's grave
In recollection of an old reproof.

(He moves off but Bellamori springs from the doorway and stabs Vitelli who falls.)

BELL. The curse of peace go with thee!

(Before he can repeat the blow Francesca rushes out and interposes.)

FRAN. Savoy! Savoy! Savoy!

(Enter an Officer and Soldiers—some the Duke's men, some Free Lances.)

FRAN. The General Vitelli has been murdered!

Here is the man.

(She faints. The Lances go to plunder the body of Vitelli. The Duke's Soldiers at a sign from the Officer approach Bellamori.

OFFICER. Our General murdered, sure enough! Seize that villain!

What! are these carrion crows preying on the body of our own general? These ruffians would murder their mother if she swallowed a scudi. Level your pikes men; charge them.

(The Lances are driven off. One of them finds a paper in Vitelli's breast. One of the Soldiers brings this paper to the officer. Bellamori is led off.

FR. Now he is dead; what more?

UB. Thou art a heroine.

FR. Thy mission hath its end. I know thy history.

UB. My history!

FR. I heard it from his wife.

UB. His *wife.* Is she his *wife!*

FR. *Which* is the murderer?

UB. Whatever guilt there is, is mine. I've done it.

I charged my follower, if I should fail,

To strike the blow for me.

FR. And he has done it—

UB. Yes.

FR. *Thy peace is gone!* (*Exit.*)

UB. Lady, a word. Oh! listen! She is gone. (*Exit.*)

OFFICER. (*looking at paper.*) If every dead man's epitaph were to be compiled on an authentic document of that sort, faith we should be all ashamed to go into a graveyard to see what would be seen; and the disgrace of dying would frighten many a scoundrel into longevity. But it is a good document for me— that it is - a good document for me! The stabbing fellow did not mean this; yet, it is a pity to hang him. Won't the Duke open his eyes? Won't he? ·(*Exit.*)

[END OF THIRD ACT.]

———•———

ACT IV.

SCENE 1.—*The Ducal Palace—Enter Duke, Chancellor Mancini and three councillors.*

DUKE. (*Holding a paper.*) I have assembled you my councillors,
On this the eve of our great enterprise,
To make unto your ears some revelations
Which I've deferred till now.   Three days ago,
As you and all the people know already,
An officer—than whom none higher stood
In our esteem or the command he bore,
Both which it will appear were much too high—
Was wounded by a man named Bellamori,
Who with Uberto hither came from Florence.
Thy noble girl, Mancini, rushed between them.
Before proceeding further, I would ask
What has been told to you by the commissioners
Who were to know Vitelli's state of health ?
  FIRST COUNCILLOR. His wound seems mortal.
  DUKE. I am sorry for it.
  SECOND COUN. 'Tis a poor end for such great qualities.
  THIRD COUN. It looks like a loss !
  DUKE. (*To Mancini.*)   What dost thou say ?
  MANCINI. I never liked the man.
  DUKE.   Then as I live,
Thy evidence would be more welcome to us
Than evidence like this (*holding the paper.*)
              That very day,
Uberto came to me with explanation
Both of the cause and manner of this deed.
He said Vitelli wronged him formerly
In ways to which I gave but little heed.
Uberto made revenge his sole life-business,
And in that business took a potent partner
Named Bellamori.
  1ST COUN.   Then we see it all.
He took his hire, and did Uberto's work.
  DUKE. There are more windings in this simple matter,
Than simple people think of.   When Uberto
Came to my service, he was ignorant
That his good friend Vitelli came before him.
Finding him here, he felt constrained in honor
To spare until our enterprise was finished,
A man whom I had vested with importance.
'Twas accident that solely did the rest ;
And yet Uberto thinks that on himself,
Lies all the weight and guilt of killing him.
But I, informed by other lights, assured him
That his was but a secondary part ;

That in my eyes the actors in this matter
Were only Bellamori and Vitelli.
   MANC. My lord, the light by which thou hast been guided
Shines from that paper.
   DUKE   Now I come to it.
This paper marked all o'er with blood and treason,
When liberated by the sudden steel,
Leaped like remorse from out Vitelli's bosom.
Here has he covenanted with the French,
To give them an admission on the Alps ;
And for reward they are to make him duke
Of the best portion of our patrimony.
Were he not struck in time the deed were done.
And this arh-fiend of treason, in one week
Had built our very hearth-stones into walls
To shut us out forever from our homes.
     (*They pass around the paper.*)
   FIRST COUN. Never was murderous blow so fraught with justice!
   SECOND COUN. The devil was here divided with himself.
The crime has worked as though the best intention
Plotted our welfare.
   THIRD COUN.   'Twas a blessed crime—
   MANC. A deed for which the doer must be hanged,
By those whom he has saved   a guilty benefit!
   DUKE. Ye look on matters with no statesmen's eyes,
Stupidity ! ye talk of guilt and murder.
These names have fearful penalties attached.
Ye would not have me lop the hand that served me ?
   FIRST COUN. It were unjust !
   SECOND COUN.   A crime !
   THIRD COUN. This soldier must have known Vitelli's purpose.
   DUKE. There is the truth I wish to see established.
   MANC. But if he should disown it.
   DUKE.   Question him,
And if it doth appear as we would wish,
Then shall he be rewarded as he merits.
Yet, I am sorry for Vitelli's death ;
For 'tis not *merely* death that he should suffer.
   FIRST COUN. Torture were strictly merited by him.
   DUKE. And torture he should have—bring in the prisoner.
  (*One of the Councillors goes to the side and beckons—enter
      guard with Bellamori.*
   DUKE. (*To Manc.*) Put thou the question.
   MANC. Thou call'st thyself a soldier ? Is it so ?
   BELL. I have led soldiers e're I've seen Savoy.
   MANC. Then was it soldierly, when on thy post,
To wait in ambush for the general
And as he passed to slay him—
   BELL.   A mistake!
I was not on a military post,

But waiting for my leader—'twas my privilege.
As he passed by he so reviled my name,
I rushed and struck him—'twas my privilege.
  MAN. This is a privilege not granted here
To soldiers or to any.
  FIRST COUN. Why did Vitelli use such terms of thee?
  BELL. Because I understood him —
  DUKE.   There's the question.
  BELL. Once I was in a melancholy plight,
Away in Naples, in our baron's castle :
I was commander; but to say the truth,
Since none but lords and princes hear the tale
Whose ears are safe—I had no troops at all.
At this he questions me as if I had.
'Fore God, the curse of peace was bad enough,
Without his compliments.
  MAN.   The curse of peace!
He says it in the hearing of the prince.
  DUKE. Peace which all princes love and make their study.
  MAN. And which to make secure they draw the sword!
  DUKE. (*Looking at the paper.*) Evil came more within his
        sphere than good?
  BELL. It did, my lord.
  DUKE.   This paper fell from him?
  BELL. There's nothing charitable, good or truthful
In that same paper.
  DUKE.   ʹ   'Tis clear as light,
Thou didst suspect him ere thou gavest the blow.
  BELL. There's treachery in that paper—is there not?
                              (*Enter Uberto.*)
  UB. My lord, I have craved entrance at this time,
To make one effort more to save this soldier.
(*Bellamori makes dumb show to Uberto who does not heed
    him.*)
  BELL. The soldier must make efforts to save *thee*.
  UB. I can not wear the mask his love has woven.
  BELL. (*Aside.*) He makes a rope, with one end for himself and
      ⁻ me upon the other.
  UB. Put nothing in the record of this deed
But vengeance · and put after it my name.
  BELL. (*Aside.*) 'Twont suit—the paper yet will save us both.
  DUKE. Here is a record where thy name is absent.
Here has Vitelli bargained with the French
To let them on the Alps when we are gone.
  UB. O Heavens!
  DUKE.   Mine is much the graver charge—
Were he not dead he'd feel how grave it was.
But now the only thing that we can do
Is to give due reward to Bellamori,
Who knew his guilt, and knowing punished it.

UB. (*aside.*) He knew it! Crooked are the ways of courts,
And crooked-minded those that walk in them!

BELL. Whene'er I draw my dagger on a man, I know my man ;
I know what can convict him ; and all the courts and judges of
the world need not acquit him after.

DUKE. Bellamori,
Since he must die, we will reward thy duty
And give thee proper rank—but first remember
Thy privileges must be all abandoned.

BELL. And for the rank to be bestowed, my lord,
I'd not ambition to be more than Captain.

DUKE. Then Captain Bellamori, now depart!
Thou shalt see war to-morrow.

BELL. I wonder is there any Naples' wine
In these strange places! . (*Exit.*)

DUKE. Ere we part to-morrow,
We will find out if yet Vitelli lives.
If so, put up the rack within this hall—
We'll show our estimate of his offence.
If he is dead, then heaven had mercy on him.
(*Exit Duke, Mancini and Council.*)

UB. Here's no revenge, although the deed is mine—
But all the bitterness that sated vengeance
Is sure to know. Francesca, O Francesca!
There is one angel in this darksome world,
And thou art she. (*Exit.*)

SCENE 2.—*The Plaza del Castello. Enter Bellamori slight-
ly drunk, followed by a crowd of soldiers cheering.*)

BELL. I hope I am proceeding with proper circumspection in
these delicate affairs. I have an idea in my mind that will aston-
ish some people. But first of all where was I? Oh! yes. Who
knows Marco Tracco? Has any one seen Marco Tracco? Can
any body tell where Marco Tracco lives?
Men!

SOLDIERS. Yes, noble Captain. (*They cheer.*)

BELL. If you see a person calling himself Marco Tracco, proceed with due circumspection, but instantly set on him, and bring
him to me and let me see him. Do you hear?

SOLDIERS. Yes, Captain.

BELL. (*To one of the soldiers.*) Are *you* Marco Tracco?

SOL. Oh! no, Captain; I am not.

BELL. (*To another.*) Are you?

SOL. No, no, Captain. No, no, no, no.

BELL. Then leave me till I call upon you. (*Exeunt soldiers.*)
I think his highness would prefer to have Vitelli living than dead.
Well, that must be seen to.
(*Enter Bonita and Pietro.*)

BONITA AND PIETRO (*Falling on their knees and crying.*)
Oh! general, pardon, pardon!

BELL. General, ha! Pardon for what?

PIETRO. For being alive, valiant general.

BON. It is great presumption in us to be alive, when so many conquering men and great robbers are in the city.

BELL. Robbers, no -caution! caution!

PI. But there will be peace soon, and they will all repent.

BELL. Peace! Why?

PI. Because Vitelli has fallen by thy valorous hand in an attempt to capture the Duke--so we are told.

BON. At the head of seventeen hundred lances; and that, after a hard battle.

BELL. Ha! good – you have heard that! However, things are not at so bad a pass yet that we are to have peace.

BON. Then, general, give us a guard to leave the city. We are afraid to go forth. I intend to go home and get married.

BELL. Ha! Married.

PI. It is necessary for us to have a man of valor at our little inn to terrify the plunderers that live upon us.

BELL. Ha! And you?

BON. Some protection is needful. The *name* of such a one might be enough. But I think I know a friend who will be there in person.

PI. Yes, indeed   we know such a friend.

BELL. Mar –

PI. Co—

BON. Tracco —

BELL. May the eternal infamy of a lasting and obscure peace surround him, cling to him and overwhelm him!

PIETRO. Amen!

BONITA. (*weeping.*) Amen.

BELL. (*aside.*) To a man of my keen generalship and habit of circumspection, a mistake like matrimony is out of the question, especially at this crisis. And yet if I do not take this step, that fellow will cut me out. If she would only betray him into my hands, I would get some of our men of high principle to kidnap him and bring him to the campaign. Bonita!

BON. General!

BELL. What sort of person is this Marco Tracco?

BON. Very handsome, splendid—but a man of few words.

BELL. Could you let me see him?

BON. That depends whether before or after I am married to—

BELL. Married to—

BON. Married to—

BELL. Oh! I see. Caution! If I am in question,
Then *after the campaign* is the word.

BON. (*aside.*) And in the meantime he wishes to lay hands on Marco, perhaps, to carry him off to the war. That would never do. I am done with this soldier. Well, I will let you see him, general.

BELL. Before we leave?

BON. Before you leave.

Pi. Take care, take care, Bonita!

Bon. All is right, father. You shall see him general.

Bell. Excellent! Now, retire to a place of safety. Here, soldiers. (*Enter two soldiers.*) (*Aside.*) This stay-at-home silent man will soon find himself in a campaign.

Bon. (*Aside*). I will let our soldier see that I am to have a husband.

Bell. (*To soldiers.*) Conduct my friends to a place of safety.

Pi. Good-bye, General!

Bon. Good-bye, General—(*aside*)—for ever.
(*Exeunt Bonita and Pietro with soldiers.*)

Bell. I've said it, and I'll say it now again,
Since caution need not check my tongue in this,
That the best signs of greatness in a prince
Are first, to give a just reward to merit,
And next to make a stirring, glorious war
And hand it down to his posterity!
Where are ye soldiers—come, step here, tall fellow—
I will use double caution in the future.
(*First Soldier steps forward.*)
Art thou a cautious man, sir?

Second S. (*Aside to third Soldier.*)
Our Captain takes in caution with his liquor.

First S. (*To Bellamori.*)
Sir, I'm sober—
If that doth not mean caution, I can change it;
I'm willing to be taught, and that is much.

Third S. (*aside to second Soldier.*)
This caution is a necessary thing.

Second S. to Third S. In truth I wish we had a bottleful!

Bell. to First S. What nature gave not can not be acquired.
Now look at me, sir—what I am at present
I was when I was born—I'm nature's work.

Second S. to Third S. For certain *grace* had nought to do with him.

First S. to Bell. Caution was in the house when thou wert born.

Second S. to Third S. So much of it, the baby got a share.

Bell. to First S. I know not, sir, what thou canst mean by that,
Caution was in the house—like a commodity—
A drug, that could be bought, sold, changed about.

First S. I might so speak, sir, of a thing transmitted from father unto son.

Bell.   'Tis well explained.

Second S. to Third S. His father was a man quite full of caution.

Third S. to Second S. He was more cautious than was prudent for him.

First S. to Bell. Is caution, sir, as needful for the soldier as for the officer?

Bell.   'Tis good for all.

5

FIRST S. to BELL. How much, sir, at a time ought one to take?
SECOND S. to THIRD S. Faith this is over-bold—this may grow
serious.
THIRD S. to SECOND S. He'd better keep a distance from his knife.
BELL. to FIRST S. God's mercy! what a question?   How much
caution?
Ye Savoyards can talk of everything
As if 'twere in a bottle on a shelf—
The time of the Free Lances is no more.
FIRST S. to BELL. Does caution, sir, put spirit in a man,
Or does it take his spirit all away?
SECOND S. to FIRST S. 'Tis spirit that put caution in a man.
BELL. to FIRST S. Now, now, do not oppress me with thy
questions:
One word for all—a soldier should have caution,
But if he should be overcharged with it,
Then he grows helpless for all active work.
SECOND S. to FIRST S. Now that's as true as that he stabbed
Vitelli.
BELL. I will not hear these questions any more,
But cleave the chaps of him who troubles me.
Ah! but my privilege is taken from me.
My men, I have a work to-day in hand
Which most of all has need of cautious men.
'Tis for this work I've called you—follow me!
Are these here cautious men?   Come hither, sirs.
SECOND and THIRD S. Come to him.
SECOND S. Captain, I've not been cautious for a week.
THIRD S. Nor I for a whole month, I dare be sworn.
BELL. Silence—and wait till you are spoken to.
I have a certain thought now in my mind,
Which may work good for all of us.   Come hither!
Meet me at midnight near Vitelli's house,
And let no one pass in without the watchword:
And for the watchword!   What shall be the watchword?
FIRST S. *Caution*, Captain.
ALL. To Vitelli's house.
SCENE 3.—*An apartment in Vitelli's house— Vitelli sleeping
on a couch, a doctor standing over him—enter Regina.*
REG. Thou say'st that he will live!   Reverse that sentence!
Say death, death—kindly death—the friend
That with his merciful and timely arrow,
Anticipates the harsher stroke of justice,
And leaves the victim to the kind construction
Of charity.   For this is not yet proved—
And death would take him from the pain, the shame,
The horror which the duke prepares for him.
Oh! think of it!   The cruel rack awaits him.
His wounded body shall be laid upon it,
And with an ingenuity most shocking

He shall be torn to pieces. Hear my prayer!
And may that heaven that will requite us all
Remit for thee that final agony,
Which, guilty that we are, awaits our end.
Go to the duke—go now—go instantly—
Say that Vitelli is before that bar
That heeds no human judgment—say he's dead.
Thou art so honored, trusted, they'll believe thee ;
The hurry of this war, the sudden march,
The press of time—all, all will aid our purpose.
And for an evidence, a paltry proof,
Of my immense, my boundless gratitude,
I'll give thee jewels, gold, a shining treasure,
The hoardings of his life. One little word
Shall make thee peer of princes. Go, good doctor,
Save, save him by thy word. We'll leave this realm ;
And in the harmless, pulseless, silent depths
Of our obscurity, we live henceforth.
Save, not his life, that is unwished for now ;
But save him from that outrage too severe
For any crime to merit—too unfit
For any mind's invention, or for the endurance
Of any criminal—save him from the rack!   (*Exit doctor.*)
There's so much gained—if heaven but be so kind
As to keep off those cruel, heartless men,
Whose vigilance sees ever their own interest
In the hard stretch of law to faults of others. (*Enter Francesca.*)
Francesca, there is one poor chance of safety ;
The doctor, yielding to my words, has gone
Unto his highness to make attestation
That he is dead ; if they depart to-morrow
In this belief, the rack is thus escaped,
And in postponement will come future means
Of safety.
    FRAN.   It is well ; you may fly both.
    REG. Ah! every sound is like a fatal message
To tell me all is useless. What was that ?
It thrilled me like the footfall of a spy.
If they should come before the doctor's errand
Is finished with the duke, what must I do ?—
Except to kill him with my woman's hands,
And show his body - (*weeping.*)
    FRAN.   Hear him how he raves!
    REG. Alas! these three days past he has been speaking
Such words, as make his guilt more plain than ever ;
And I with loathing ears have sat and listened
Unto the doubts, the hopes, the many wiles
Of his ambition.
    FRAN. 'Twas his leading passion,
    REG. And if a man makes up his mind for guilt,

What thought more worthy to engage his mind,
Or what more proper to excuse his guilt,
Than this same passion! I take pride in him—
He is no sordid criminal.
    FRAN.   Alas!
The measure of our minds must be the standard
By which to find how much we're culpable.
With all the force of his large mind he sinned—
    REG. Oh! listen! listen!
    VIT.   See them! They are going,
Away, away—and in the air above them
There is a coronet—now it descends:
My hand can touch it. Who dares hold me back?
Refrain, thou villain! It is mine—'tis mine.
I've won it and I'll grasp it, though my hand
Should wither at the touch. Ah! he has wounded me.
Slain at the moment of my victory—
When I might show myself, as I would wish.
Oh! it is hard, hard, hard—there are my friends
Almost in sight—the French, the French, the French. (*starts up.*)
Have I been dreaming? If without such dreams
Sleep cannot come, then may I wake for ever!
But it is nothing—nothing. I am strong;
Recovered—ah! is this my wife? Indeed,
This is the woman in whose cause I suffer.
Love hath an arrow, jealousy a dagger,
And *I* have felt them both. Lady Francesca,
Art thou a watcher, too, beside my couch?
If health had not outbid thee for my capture,
I might ere this, consigned by thy sweet care,
Be laid at Heaven's gate.
    FRAN.   Health is not life.
    VIT. Ah! this is moody doctrine, chilly comfort,
To cheer a friend returning from the grave.
And thou, too, my fair wife, why stand'st thou there
With head bent down and white despairing visage?
I know we have not always had that peace,
Accommodation and propriety
Which model marriages are wont to offer.
But thou dost know full well that not through me
Is overbearing, has this want appeared;
But rather through thy fault who wouldst not keep
Those vows, that with such heat thou didst insist
In making to the minister of God.
    REG. Let us be friends!   Henceforth there's peace between us.
I will amend the failures I have shown;
The duty that I swore, I will exhibit.
    VIT. Well, this is stranger still. If I were doomed
This day to death, I'd fancy *that* might call for
A revolution wonderful as this.

All goes on well—the savage hand that struck me
Had better will than skill. Has he been seized?
REG. He has not yet been seized.
VIT.   'Tis left for me.
The barbarous giant must be hunted down.
To-morrow's light shall find me on his track.
I'll show thee thy knight's squire when I have done!
REG.   Listen, Vitelli:
And while I speak I will constrain my soul
To calmness. Bellamori is not punished,
Nor will he e'er be punished.
VIT.   Why is this?
Why should he not be punished? I will rend him,
As sure as I behold to-morrow's light.
That he as yet is free, may be explained—
The time is short—a day—how long is it?
The fever that has left me so relieved,
Makes all its reign a blank.
REG. A day! *Three days.*
FRAN.   Three days since thou wert wounded.
VIT. Have I been three days lying on that couch
And your hands, every body's hands, about me?
REG. I see no terror consequent on that.
(*Vitelli tears open his breast, and not finding the paper, falls
  on the couch.*)
VIT. Merciful God! Is this done by thy hand?
Lady Francesca! Come, Regina, come:
I've lost a paper—search ye through the house
And find it for me—'tis of no importance—
Well, I won't lie, it is of some importance;
But to me only—look ye not upon it!
Bring it to me: I'll never sleep nor rest,
Breathe free, nor to myself or others
Give scope of happiness till it is found.
I'm weak—I can not move—go, go—go both,
Find me the paper. I'll do anything,
I'll do all you may ask, but find the paper.
REG. (*Aside.*) I have no heart to tell him that this paper
Is in the duke's possession.
FRAN.   Do not tell him,
But let us feign to look for it. (*Exeunt Francesca and Regina.*)
VIT. Could they have taken it from out my breast
When I lay wounded; those despoiling beasts,
Those pests of Italy, the Lances?
Or has Regina hidden or destroyed it?
Or, with a treachery worse still than my own,
Transferred it to the duke?
No, no—this can not be—she is too proud
To see her husband punished as a felon.
If she has found it, and not so consigned it,
  5*

Then am I safe—safe—safe. But ah! there's something—
Something within, that bids me fear the worst.
And if 'tis thus, if I'm defeated, foiled,
And if the brilliant glories that allured me
Are all to sink into the shadowy chasm
Of nothingness, where I shall follow them.
If punishment awaits me, and the grave,
Which never flesh did enter willingly,
Opens its mouth beneath me, with its legends
Thereafter to be proved or be refuted ;
If these make up the end of my career,
Then wherefore was I given this great ambition,
This courage to go on, this firm resolve,
This callous heart, this inborn faith of greatness
Which seemed like a decree ? Had I succeeded,
It would have been to benefit mankind,
Such as they are, not to set up a tyranny.
Now I am fallen, how shall I, all amazed,
Go through the rest of my disordered course?
Be then my nerves firm strung, my flesh all iron!
Let me be different from other men !
There is a rule for me they cannot fathom.
Let them assail me! Not a thousand racks,
No, not ten thousand fiends, shall draw one tear,
One sigh, one weak unworthy prayer from me
To shame my former self.
　　　　(*Enter Regina and Francesca—knocking outside.*)
　Reg. Alas! Vitelli, dost thou hear that noise ?
　Vit. I have no ear for it. Where is the paper ?
　Reg. Alas! I know not. I have never seen it.
　Fran. They must have found that paper on thy person.
　Reg. If there is guilt in it—
　Vit.　　　　　　　　　If there *were* guilt
I would not stoop to own it.
　Reg.　　　　　　　　Nobly spoken !
Better to die suspect than self-condemned.
Now I can die with thee, Vitelli.
(*She goes towards him, but he repulses her—more knocking.*)
　Fran. Do not despair. There is a hope remaining,
And I will try what refuge may be found
In desperation.　　　　　　　　　　　(*Exit.*)
　Reg. Vitelli, O my husband, hope is dead—
The duke has read that paper—Bellamori
Has been rewarded for the blow he gave thee.
They think thee dead ; but if they find thee living,
Thy punishment awaits thee. Hark! they come.
　Vit. Then, get my sword—I'll die where now I stand.
When I am dead, then be my friend ; proclaim
Vitelli justified in his ambition
To rule the creatures, who are named as men.

(Bellamori and soldiers burst in.)
BELL. Signor, we are glad to see thee well.
The duke expects thy company.   Arrest him!
REG. Oh! torture—torture.

[END OF FOURTH ACT.]

———◦◦———

ACT V.

SCENE 1.—*The Suburbs—enter Francesca and Uberto.*
UBERTO. Pardon a stranger's boldness in thus asking
The privilege to say farewell to thee!
FRAN. Is it for virtue that thou goest to fight?
UB. I fight for something better than a name;
There *is* no virtue; I contend for hate.
FRAN. Yes, there is virtue; and while virtue lives,
'Twere shame to give allegiance to aught else.
UB. I have not seen her—show me where she dwells;
Where is the chosen one that gives her shelter?
FRAN. Were virtue banished from all human hearts,
She does not live the less.
UB.   But so far off,
She can't protect the fools that fain would serve her.
FRAN. Her meanest favor is a richer prize
Than the black hate that rankles in thy breast.
UB. Where I gave love at first, I got back hate;
Men deal in nothing else, the choice is theirs.
FRAN. And yet I have of late seen love, devotion—
Love which hung sadly o'er the mangled form
Of one before despised, but who became
When judgment overtook him, pity's guest.
Yes; 'twas not love but pity—heavenly pity,
Which took aversion's place when guilt was suffering.
Oh! turn it in thy thoughts, canst thou desire
To chase with further woe that wretched wife?
UB. With me she ranks the same as all mankind,
I do not love her less nor hate her more.
FRAN. It is not possible to hate mankind.
Thou canst not hate thy mother.
UB.   I have none.
Thank Heaven I have no mother.
FRAN.   If thou hadst
I'd go, I'd pray to her upon my knees,
To build again that temple of thy soul,
Which thou hast left to wreck.
UB.   Were she not dead,
I'd still believe in goodness; but she's gone,
And I have never gazed on virtue since.

FRAN. Turn but thine eyes upon thy former self,
And thou canst see it yet.
UB.   And who art thou
That hast a mission to direct me thus?
FRAN. A stranger, a mere stranger, I will own,
Who oversteps all cold and narrow bounds
Through sympathy.
UB.   Through sympathy?
FRAN.   With thee.
What hast thou done?—that perjured man, Vitelli,
Drew down upon himself the wrath of Heaven,
And when its sword hung o'er him, thou didst dare
To interpose thy paltry grief and smite him.
UB. I am no better than the rest of men;
At first I thought I was, but 'twas an error.
FRAN. Thou art in error still, in error worse!
UB. Ha! what could I have done?   The fault was theirs—
Is theirs who made me what I am—a wretch.
FRAN. One thing thou couldst have done.
UB.   And that,
FRAN.   Forgiven.
UB. Forgive them!
FRAN.   If thou didst, thou hadst been happy.
UB. Forgive them!   If I did I had been senseless.
'Twere but to win contempt with injury,
And make my agonies the jest of malice.
FRAN. The sufferer's dignity endures all wrong,
While malice pois'ning ev'ry feeble shaft
From its own guilty life, feels hourly torture.
UB. A debt was due which vengeance could extort.
FRAN. Then vengeance spoke thee false, and led thee false.
Did vengeance place thee where thou wert at first?
UB. And could forgiveness place me where I stood?
FRAN. No, but 'twould lift thee higher: yet forgive;
I ask thee for thy mother's sake, *forgive!*
UB. He's dead, and let him be.
FRAN.   If so, forgive him.
'Tis not for him I ask, but for thyself.
Hast thou e'er asked thyself, since that dread night
"*He's dead—what more?*"
UB.   I have:
FRAN.   And what remains?
UB. I know not what remains.
FRAN.   Then I will tell thee.
An image of thyself and one of him.
The image of thyself is of one fall'n,
Cast down, degraded from a noble height;
His image, swathed in a bloody shroud,
Puts on the dignity that thou hast lost,
And ever moves beside it, moves there now.

Was it not better when he injured thee,
To let him pass away from sight and mind,
And keep thy sight and mind pure as at first,
Than thus to have thy eyes and mem'ry plagued?
    UB. Away! thy words do but create the picture:
I see it, but 'twill vanish when thou'rt gone.
    FRAN. Do not deceive thyself, it will not vanish.
I did not make it, I but gave its meaning.
Thy proud misanthropy may bear thee up;
But underneath the surface lies remorse.
There is a germ of love in ev'ry heart
Which, if once stifled, as it was by thee,
Converts that heart into a viler thing
Than e'er it hated.
    UB.   Can it be remorse?
Am I the wrong-doer—the criminal?
Have I, to pay a wrong which should be pardoned,
Outpour'd a rancor which can't hope for pardon.
If 'twas to tell me this such pains were taken,
Then pains are thrown away—I am made wise;
And thy benev'lence is no more than mine.
    FRAN. Heaven knows if I could tell thee what would raise thee,
Raise thee to what thou wert ere sorrow met thee,
Recall the happiness that once was thine,
And give it an irrevocable stamp,
That would I do?
    UB. Then tell me one thing only. Say, " He lives."
                              (*Enter Regina.*)
    REG. He's gone—they've taken him—can I endure it?
    UB. (*Aside.*) He's buried in the earth; so shall I be.
    REG. Let it be told to all who knew Regina,
She took a malefactor to her arms,
But in his agony she pitied him.
    FRAN. (*Aside.*) Vitelli is discovered. Peace, Regina!
    REG. Ye heavens who trace in shame, in public shame,
The punishment that's due to my caprice,
There is the teacher who is sent by you
To point its rigid meaning. O, Uberto,
Thy slight is well avenged, too well avenged,
To weigh the paltry wrong thou hast endured.
Surely thou canst not count it as a wrong
To be deprived of me.
    UB.   Of all frivolities,
The worst is that which shows through our distress.
    REG. Frivolity and I long since have parted.
I come an humble victim to thy hate,
Take then my life; but, as thou takest it,
Thou wilt be kind not cruel.
    UB.   What is done
Has not produced such joy within my breast,

That I would do it twice.

REG. Then come with me.
There, take my hand : we'll see the sight together.
Since thou canst feel, 'twill make excuse for me.

UB. Where wouldst thou go ?

REG.   I thought ye knew it all.

FRAN. Regina, go thyself, we'll follow thee.

UB. (*Aside.*) Now if I thought this madness were put on
To conquer me—

REG. Alone, alone—I shall be there alone.
And when he's gone, my lonely thoughts will paint him,
Will paint him as my eyes shall shortly see him.
Oh! cruel, cruel, cruel—see they bring him !   (*Exit Regina.*)

UB. Uttered by other and more reasoning lips,
These words might move me ;
But she has proved herself a heartless woman.

FRAN. Not heartless, but perverse ; but there's a meaning
In these her words too dreadful for the ear.

UB. She means his death.

FRAN.   Would that it were his death.

UB. What! does Vitelli live ?

FRAN.   Say thou dost wish it.

UB. Yes, since thy words disclosed to me myself.

FRAN. Vitelli lives.

UB.   That is a victory
More precious than the triumphs I have gained,
Dearer than all the lives I've spared or taken.

FRAN. But ah! this boon of life which gives thee joy
Brings double bitterness and shame for him.

UB. The duke will punish him?

FRAN.   Most dreadfully.
Regina's words were true ; they bring him hither;
Let us stand by and watch them as they pass.

    (*Enter Bellamori and a guard conducting Vitelli.*)

VIT. Stay for a moment, there is time enough :
Thou Bellamori, hast displayed a malice
In thy officiousness I cannot fathom.
It looks so needless, this that thou hast done.

FRAN. How proudly, yet how feelingly he speaks !

UB. Even from my heart I pardon him !

VIT. Let me reflect a moment !

(*Enter from behind Pietro, Bonita, and a queer-looking person who has on his back a box, on which is written Marco
Tracco.*)

PI. (*Aside.*) This appears to be our soldier once more, and he
is leading the signor to the torture. As she *is* such a little jilt, I
am glad she has not jilted a quiet, peaceable man. It is well, too,
that Marco knows nothing at all about him.

BON. Now, Marco, since we've found each other in the city, we
will end our visit, for 'tis a cruel place. See, what a sight!

PI. We know some of these parties don't we daughter?

BON. Oh! see that noble signor going to the torture, and that tall savage that guards him so securely.

PI. When you and Marco are married, you won't remember anything about it.

BON. We cannot be married without going home, and they stand right in our path.

(*They approach the soldiers. Bonita covers her face.*)

BON. Give us leave to pass, sir. We are a wedding party, and our way lies through here.

VIT. A wedding party! *I* once went on such a party, and yet my way now lies this way. It may not hinder *him* from travelling this same road some time. But, no, no, he is a wretched fellow and can never travel such a path as this. *A wretched fellow!* In the lexicon of ambition there is no such word as *truth*.

BELL. Pass on!

BON. (*To Marco as they pass.*) Say it now, silent man, as we go by!

(*As they go through, the name on the box becomes visible to Bellamori.*

MARCO. What a bloody-minded person that soldier seems to be, Ha! Ha!

BON. Now, do you think so?

(*Bellamori makes a movement to seize Marco, but again looks to his prisoner and gives up the idea.*)

VIT. Here you, girl of the inn, here is a purse for thy wedding-day. When that happy idiot by thy side takes out the coins, he may find ambition amidst them. So, if Vitelli's curse be entailed on ye both, remember also Vitelli's caution. (*Throws purse.*)

BON. Thanks, signor. We will pray for thee! But bless you, Marco has no need for such anxieties. *I* am going to be the manager.

MAR. Is it time to say it again? What a bloody-minded villain that soldier seems to be!

BON. Really, do you think so?

MAR. A bloody-minded villain!

(*Bellamori makes another movement to capture Marco, but fearing to lose his prisoner, stops short.*)

BON. Good-bye, signor!

PI. Good-bye, signor!

BON. (*To Marco.*) Speak, silent man, speak to the signor.

MAR. A bloody-minded villain!

BON. (*Pushing him.*) No, no. You must be taught.
(*Exeunt Marco, Pietro and Bonita.*)

VIT. Lead on! I'll see the duke about this matter.
(*Exeunt soldiers, Bellamori and Vitelli.*)

UB. They take him to the torture?

FRAN. To the torture!

UB. But yet the prince may hear him and acquit him.

FRAN. He will not hear one word; his fate is certain.

Ub. I would it could be changed!

Fran. Try then, and change it;
Show the divinest power that man can show—
The power of forgiving.

Ub. I will try.

Fran. And there's not one who wears the form of man,
But midst the crimes and errors of this world,
Will yet rejoice to be remotely like thee.

Ub. There is no height so rugged but I'd scale,
Didst thou persuade me thus.   (*Exeunt.*)

Scene 2.—*The great hall in the duke's palace – a dark curtain
concealing a rack and executioner. Enter the duke, chancellor, and three councillors, Regina and her father Jerome.*

Duke. Old man, what is thy plea? Bring in the pris'ner!
  (*Vitelli is brought in by Bellamori with guard.*)

Vit. I did not think to see thee here, good father!
This is a formidable hall of audience;
My retinue is somewhat of the fiercest!

Jer. Accursed be thy lightness, selfish man,
Which thus can end for thee, for me, for her
In irredeemable disgrace. But O kind prince,
Grant me a boon in pity for my age,
Not through compassion for this arch deceiver;
His sorrowing wife, is my long-sought-for child –
My wild, capricious, but still virtuous child.
Let not her innocent descendants, born
In the unwholesome shadow of the rack,
Like blighted flowers shed bane upon a house,
Where shame hath never come!

Duke.   These words have power
With those who contravening nature's laws,
Have set aside thy fatherly direction:
They have a power with *her* to make her weep
Her ill-considered choice – they have *no* power
With *me* to make me change my sovereign justice.

Vit. Justice is on the rack – I've heard her shriek:
She is the criminal at every bar,
And not the ruling power.

Reg. My lord, he may be innocent – have pity!
He could not, would not do this: if he dared
To plot the treach'ry that is charged against him,
Then here is one that would expose him first,
Though he were dearer than the dearest idol,
That maiden ever cherished in her heart.

Duke. This speaks for thee—canst say aught good of him?

Reg. I can! I can! Oh! he was kind to me.
Let not the bloody engine of disgrace,
Receive my husband.

Duke.   Madame, all is vain.
Were he *less* kind to thee and *more* to me,

There was a balance that would tell for him.
Look at this record, written with his hand,
Which tears in partial eyes may shut from view,
But which the scrutinizing glance of justice,
Sees in its native horror.
 REG.   Cruel prince,
And is not death enough? Must life be tortured?
Will it not serve to send him to be judged
With limbs unracked before the bar of God?
Or wilt thou dare forestall that dread decision
With previous petty cruelty?
 DUKE.   Enough!
I sit not here to be reproved or questioned.
Now shall my power find measure for his guilt,
Not, I avow to Heaven, so much to punish,
As to make known to daring malefactors,
That their triumphant magnitude of guilt
May almost be outdone by princes' punishments:
I ask my councillors if this be just.
 COUNCILLORS. 'Tis just—let him behold!
 DUKE. Unveil the torture!
(*The curtain is drawn aside- enter Francesca and Uberto.*)
 UB. My lord, at this dread hour of rightful sentence,
I, as an injured man, would speak my thoughts.
 VIT. Still the same tale! Why 'twill outlive the world.
Can't a quick stab cross off a stale account?
Why even my wound grows old, but this is new!
 DUKE. We'll hear thee as a man whom he hath injured.
'Tis nothing good thou hast to say of him?
 UB. 'Tis nought but evil I shall say of him.
 REG. Dastard, thine is a meanness worse than any.
 UB. The evil he hath done me may look trivial,
Weighed in the scales which hold a state's concerns.
But 'tis an evil, which unless assuaged
By superhuman and subduing influence,
One man can never pardon in another.
 VIT. Is this the torture that was meant for me?
      (*To the executioner.*)
Thou mute enigma, thou art but a phantom!
It is a triumph they propose for me.
 UB. This venerable man, whom with surprise
I see at this dread hour, was my next neighbor.
Drawn towards him by respect, I learned to love him,
Since I loved her whom most he loved on earth.
Alas! for youthful eyes which seldom look
The way which wisdom's cautioning finger points,
Little I knew how blindly one may follow
The things we most dislike:
Vitelli came to see me in my home,
And I with stupid zeal invited him
6

To come to see her; with one glance around
He understood us all—
    VIT.   That's true as truth.
    UB. And with a bad ambition, which conceived
To him a triumph without happiness,
To me, a happiness forever lost,
Induced her false unloving heart to leave me.
Bent on revenge for two long years I've sought them,
Two foul betrayers of two sacred trusts,
Who dared not let the morning's light behold
Their shame, but with a sudden plunge in sin
Fled in the night.
    REG.   This was not shame, 'twas freedom.
Heaven is my judge there has been no dishonor.
Ev'n from the first I was a stainless wife.
    UB. But evil reputation followed after,
Which made his triumph seem what he designed it.
This was the tale I heard where'er I turned;
And this it is which makes him, in my eyes,
Who trusted him and took his lightest counsel,
A dark and dire offender. Yet my lord,
Coming within this court where he stood high,
I curbed my wrath, until with loyalty
I could attend to my own proper griefs.
'Twas but a chance that struck him down at length,
But yet a chance that grew from out my wrong.
    VIT. A chance entrusted to an ambush'd soldier,
One of that class that too long cursed our land,
Unwilling to be led—unfit to lead,
An ox upon the march, a wolf in plunder,
With all the vigilance of an assassin,
And all the sluggishness of a poltroon.
My lord, heed not such men, but heed my oath.
    DUKE. My ears are closed to thee. Conclude Uberto!
    UB. After those others, who have here petitioned,
With all my wrongs in view, I make my pray'r.
    DUKE. 'Tis well; thou cam'st to strengthen my intent
Against their importunity. I may
With safety undertake to grant thy prayer;
Thy grievances are thy most warm petition.
    JER. Uberto, thou art even as base as he.
    VIT. Let him petition! he is not a man;
He begs revenge by whining.
    DUKE.   What is it?
    UB.   Pardon him!
(*The Duke starts from his chair; Vitelli moves involuntarily,*
  but relapses into indifference.)
    UB. Because he injured me, I plead for him;
Because he outraged me, I try to save him.
I wish not that the pardon I accord him,

Should impotently rest upon his head,
But draw thy pardon with it.   Oh! forgive him.
Mar not the new-found happiness I feel
By torturing the man whom I forgive!
(*The Duke standing with face averted remains silent.   Fran-
    cesca approaches her father.*)
    FRAN. Dear father, aid him in his sublime end !
Father, sustain his prayer !
    MAN.   Great Duke, forgive him.
    FRAN. (*Kneeling to the council.*) Signors, this bright example
        unto men
May lose completeness through your want of aid ;
Or it may triumph and not owe its glory
To any words from you—speak to your prince.
    FIRST COUN. Let him be pardoned.
    SECOND COUN.   Released, but banished hence.
    DUKE. When my own councillors are thus turned traitors,
What can I do alone?   Release the culprit !
But let me not behold him, lest the sight
Make me recall what is but wrenched from me !
(*The guards release Vitelli.   Uberto takes Francesca by the
    hand and leads her towards him.   Regina takes her other
    hand and kisses it.*)
    UB. Vitelli, thank this gentle intercessor,
Who came between me and my cherished wrath,
And coming, saved us both ; saved thee from torture,
Me from a torture that would last for life.
                (*Handing him the dagger.*)
Here pass from me all signs that may bring back
Thy crime and my revenge ; now I am lightened ;
I am what once I was before we met,
Ere double error plunged me in distress.
                (*Vitelli takes the dagger.*)
    VIT. And thou shalt shine above me—I must stoop,
And for the boon of life confess myself
The meanest reptile that's possess'd of life !
I hate such givers and such gifts alike.   (*He stabs Uberto.*)
(*Commotion.   The Duke rushes to the spot.   Bellamori an-
    ticipates.*
    BELL. Make way ! The stroke is mine—let no man touch him.
I'll immolate whoever takes my prey !   (*He stabs Vitelli.*)
I should have struck this blow, thou mocking fiend,
The day thou didst presume to call me coward.
    DUKE. Rack him while he lives !
    VIT. It is too late.   I had a friend in court.   (*Dies.*)
(*Uberto striving to rise, turns round and leans upon one arm.
    He seems not to know that Vitelli is slain.*)
    UB. Vitelli, I'll not take thy pardon back.
Come here, Francesca ; once I did not think
The time would ever come when I'd be happy.

The thanks are thine that I am happy now.
A thousand daggers could not stab my peace;
Vitelli, I forgive thee, I for——give——thee.   *(Dies.)*
(Regina falls at the feet of her father between the bodies of
    Vitelli and Uberto.)
   REG. Mine, mine, the wretched fault, the bad caprice,,
That brings to view this hideous spectacle..
Not all the tears I'll shed throughout my life,
Can wash this blood—not all the care I'll give
Can e'er outweigh the wilful bad contempt
I gave thy counsels and thy high discernment.
        (Francesca kneeling by the body of Uberto.)
   FRAN. Happy this day for me were he now living,
But doubly honored- doubly dear in death.
Dear father, pardon me what I shall say;
I loved him, gentlemen; his was a heart
That had no dross within it.   Great in all things —
Great in revenge—great in his forgiveness —
The martyr of forgiveness; let his name
When all-surrounding guilt seems ev'rywhere,
And good is lost to view, arouse our hearts
To look to some such sunny eminence
As he hath gained, which shews that there are yet
Within the waste, some spots of rest we have not met..

THE END.